HUNTED WOLF

Center Point
Large Print

Also by T. T. Flynn and available from
Center Point Large Print:

A Bullet for the Utah Kid
The Resurrection Kid
Cantrell

**This Large Print Book carries the
Seal of Approval of N.A.V.H.**

HUNTED WOLF

A Western Quartet

T. T. FLYNN

CENTER POINT LARGE PRINT
THORNDIKE, MAINE

This Circle Ⓥ Western is published by
Center Point Large Print in the year 2018 in
co-operation with Golden West Literary Agency.

First Edition
August, 2018

The text of this Large Print edition is unabridged.
In other aspects, this book may vary
from the original edition.
Printed in the United States of America
on permanent paper.
Set in 16-point Times New Roman type.

ISBN: 978-1-68324-895-8

Library of Congress Cataloging-in-Publication Data

Names: Flynn, T. T., author | Flynn, T. T. Death for double-o neighbors.
Title: Hunted wolf : a western quartet / T.T. Flynn.
Description: First edition. | Thorndike, Maine :
   Center Point Large Print, 2018. | Series: A Circle V western
Identifiers: LCCN 2018015868 | ISBN 9781683248958
   (hardcover : alk. paper)
Subjects: LCSH: Western stories. | Large type books.
Classification: LCC PS3556.L93 A6 2018 | DDC 813/.54—dc23
LC record available at https://lccn.loc.gov/2018015868

Table of Contents

Death for Double-O Neighbors   7

The Out Trail   89

Powder for Santa Anna   121

Hunted Wolf   225

DEATH FOR DOUBLE-O NEIGHBORS

I

Old Bob Hurley stood in the sheriff's office like a fierce old lobo, growling his defiance. "If it'll take war to keep the homestead outfits out of my herds, I'll make war. I asked you men here to hear me say it before the sheriff . . . and it's the last time I'll say it."

A shaft of sunlight through the grimy side window splashed gold over the dusty reward posters on the back wall. Outside, the sunshine was hot, but Colonel Bob Hurley's voice held a chill Tom Lucas knew only too well.

When Old Bob talked like that, he meant what he said. Anyone who'd lived around him for a time knew that.

Tom Lucas eyed Bowlings, the fleshy sheriff, who'd rather crack a joke than make an arrest. No one could expect much from him. Lucas looked at Thomason, the restless young district attorney, smarter than a blade with his law, set for higher places than a district attorney. Bowlings looked solemn. Thomason was interested, noncommittal; his glance was flicking over the other faces, to see how they were taking it.

Pinwheel Simms, bowlegged, truculent, one of the smaller cattlemen, was scowling. Jack

O'Leary, square-shouldered owner of the Flying M, taking his cue from Simms, was also frowning. Cal Hardesty, of the N-Cross-N, was smiling thinly. And Brett Canfield, manager of the big XS syndicate, which was almost as large as Old Bob's Double-O Ranch, was sober and interested. Brett Canfield, as usual, looked as smartly dressed and aloof as one of his English syndicate owners would have been.

Thomason, the district attorney, cleared his throat. "You're being frank enough about it, Colonel Hurley. . . . Almost too frank, perhaps."

Bob Hurley shoved his hat back on his shaggy gray hair. He looked, Tom Lucas reflected, exactly like the scarred, toughened old fighter that he was. Men who worked for Old Bob Hurley would follow him to hell. Men who disliked or feared him usually respected him.

Bob Hurley's reply to Thomason started as a positive growl. "I'm showin' cards fair and open. I've complained plenty about missing cattle. My top hands aren't fools. We know there's no rustlin' bunches hanging out in these parts. We could handle 'em. In the old days we shot 'em out and kept the range around here peaceable. But these homestead outfits are bleedin' us to death. They get a few here and a few there . . . and it shows up like hell at tally time. I'll give any man beef to eat who needs it. But I'll be damned if the Hurley cows are going to build up every small herd in these parts. It'll stop from now on . . . or we'll stop it!"

Cal Hardesty sneered. "Just what'll you do, Hurley?"

"If you've never lived through a range war, Hardesty, you'll learn."

Sandy-haired, freckled Cal Hardesty gave a thin-lipped grin that seemed to split his face in half.

"Maybe you don't know it," he said, "but there's two sides to a range war. We've got law now. This ain't your private pasture. A heap of the new folks don't take to you playin' cock-of-the-walk like you've been used to doin'. Better not start anything you'll be sorry for."

Old Bob turned a bleak look on Tom Lucas. "How about you, Tom? You're one of the leaders of these small ranchers now."

Tom shrugged. "I'm trying to be fair, Colonel. I've got to be fair. I hope you'll see it. Some of these small new outfits don't amount to much, but the men who own them think they do. They don't like to be ordered about. Maybe there has been some closed-eye branding. I've been talking against it. I've seen this coming. A range war won't settle anything. It'll be suicide for the weakest outfits . . . and it won't help the big ones any. None of us can afford it."

Cal Hardesty's chortle had a raw edge of nastiness to it. "Sounds like you're a Hurley

11

man, Lucas," he said. "You was hand-raised on the Hurley Ranch. Hurley helped you get a start. It's about time you show plain where you stand."

"I stand half owner of the Wagon Wheel, Hardesty. If a range war starts, me and Latigo Blair'll be dragged into it. We want peace."

Cal Hardesty's grin was nastier. "Sure you ain't got any more reason than that?"

Pinwheel Simms grinned knowingly. So did Jack O'Leary. Bob Hurley frowned slightly.

Tom felt his face reddening. For a moment there was murder in his heart. No one but Cal Hardesty would have tried to drag Marcia Hurley into this—especially when Marcia had been away four years and was just coming back. She was coming back today.

"What you think," Tom bit out, "don't matter a damn! We all need peace. It's up to everyone to try and keep it."

Brett Canfield smiled easily. Older than Tom, but still a young man, Canfield had been a cowman all his life, although he did not look it. Canfield's ability to look like an Easterner and think like an Easterner had gained him the confidence of the syndicate which hired him.

Now Canfield spoke with the good-natured reason of an outsider. "You're all getting hot over nothing. Hurley, you can spare a few head now and then. The syndicate has lost its share. We're willing to be reasonable about it. There's enough

12

law around here to take care of any situation. The district attorney will certainly prosecute anyone caught with wet cattle."

Thomason hastily agreed. "Any time the sheriff has a case, I'll take it into court. I'm here to carry out the law without fear or favor."

A cold gleam of skepticism entered Old Bob's look. Tom could almost read the old rancher's mind. Thomason had been elected by the votes of the smaller ranchers. Thomason—and everyone else—knew what would happen if Thomason started a campaign of prosecution against the men who had put him in office. A new district attorney would be in at the next election. Passions were running high.

"I've had my say," Old Bob said shortly. "Think it over, men."

The door closed behind the old-timer's stiff back.

Cal Hardesty cursed softly, snapped: "High-handed old hellion!"

"Thinks he's God A'mighty," Pinwheel Simms snarled. " 'Bout time he's learnin' he don't rule the roost. Maybe he thinks no one's noticed he's hirin' extra men. If he can't get his way by bluff, he'll go after it with guns and hell."

Bowlings, the sheriff, was uncomfortable. "Let it ride until something happens," he said. And the district attorney nodded agreement.

Brett Canfield looked at his watch. "About

train time." He was smiling faintly. "Going over to the station, Lucas?"

"Maybe," said Tom shortly.

Tom left the sheriff's office, conscious that they were grinning at his back. They knew he'd be at the station.

The crowd at the railroad station was larger than usual.

Tom rolled a cigarette and leaned against the back of his buckboard. He was expecting some small freight. Bob Hurley's best buggy was hitched near him. Old Bob was on the platform, talking to friends as he waited for his granddaughter.

Tom's heart beat harder as a whistle wailed in the distance. . . . Marcia was coming back. She'd be different, of course. But she'd be Marcia. Life would be better for knowing Marcia was back.

The train ground to a dusty, noisy stop. Tom glimpsed Marcia coming down the steps. And then she vanished in Old Bob's hug and the press of friends around her.

Brett Canfield's gray sombrero showed in the group. Canfield had never made any bones about thinking Marcia was the prettiest girl in a week's ride.

Then Old Bob was coming toward his buggy, with Marcia holding his arm. She was looking about questioningly. She saw Tom at the buckboard, said something to her grandfather, left the others, and hurried toward the buckboard. Marcia *had* changed. She looked older, more assured— and twice as pretty. But her smile was the same.

"Hello, cowboy," she cried, and added reproachfully as she reached him, "I thought you'd be at the train steps. I was looking for you."

Tom grinned. "Didn't seem to be any room by the steps. Gosh, it's good to see you, Marcia."

Marcia still had a few freckles. Her nose had the same alluring tip-tilt. And her eyes were just as blue and warm and friendly.

"How is everything, Tom? Tell me about your new ranch. You wouldn't write me anything much."

"I knew you had too much on your mind to bother with a small cowman."

Marcia frowned with mock anger. "That isn't even an excuse, Tom. Didn't we use to talk about your plans by the hour?"

"Used to."

"We'll start again," said Marcia. "I've got to run now, Tom. You'll come over as soon as you can? The ranch won't seem the same without you."

"I'll wear a path," Tom promised, and then it was time for Marcia to go.

Bob Hurley's matched bays whirled the buggy away in a swirl of dust. And the sun seemed brighter, the day warmer, as Tom went to see about his freight.

Marcia hadn't picked up any fancy Eastern ideas during those years. The fact that she and her brother Bud would one day own the big Hurley Ranch still made no difference. Marcia was a cowman's granddaughter and a dead cowman's daughter. A thirty-a-month cowhand was as important to her as a governor.

Bud Hurley was different. Three years older than Marcia, Bud had a streak of arrogance. Old Bob, Tom knew, had tried to curb that streak in Bud, without much success.

There were other errands to do in town. Tom took his time, listening to the talk. Word of Bob Hurley's warning had spread, and it had lost nothing in the telling. Some men were indignant, some defiant.

For a good many of them, Tom suspected, the shoe fitted. Too many small homesteaders made a practice of tiding over the first lean years with strays from any big outfit close at hand. Old Bob had tried to keep the homesteaders out and had failed. He never had been able to get along with them. Old Bob could not forget the great days when his word was absolute law for a hundred miles in any direction. . . . But times were changing.

Dick Kinsley, owner of the Shorthorn Saloon and a small ranch south of town, was philosophical about it, over a glass of beer, as he stood at the head of his bar. Half a dozen customers were listening in.

"There'll be trouble . . . and damned if I want to see it," said Kinsley, a heavy-set, slow-speaking man with red veins forking over his cheeks. He pulled at his beer, wiped foam from his mustache before proceeding. "Bob Hurley's getting old and boogery. He's living in the past. He's always had his way, and he still figures to have it. But he can bring in gunmen until hell and gone . . . and he'll still have a range full of small outfits that'll be gunning for his hide. Might be different if he had a couple more big outfits to throw in with him. But he ain't. Brett Canfield's syndicate'll keep out of it. Brett Canfield's smart. He aims to have his own spread someday. He'll sit tight and let the fireworks pop. And when it's over, Brett Canfield'll be sitting on top of the heap. Everybody else'll be a loser. I sure hate to see it, but it's coming. Mark my word."

Tom nodded gloomy agreement. "If they don't let the Double-O beef alone, it'll come. Something's got to be done."

Kinsley chuckled drily. "You better think fast then."

The swinging doors burst open at that moment. Tom swung from the bar as he recognized Latigo Blair, his partner. Tall, gaunt, with a drooping mustache, a weathered face, sharp eyes, bristly brows, and long arms, Latigo was red with anger.

"We're burnt out, Tom! Haystack, house, and bunkhouse!"

Latigo thrust out an arm. Blood had soaked through the shirt sleeve.

"Pete Salazar was there with me," he said hoarsely. "But they was down on us before we knowed what happened."

"Who did it, Latigo?" But Tom knew before Latigo answered.

"Who you think? Double-O gunmen! Bud Hurley led 'em! He spouted some damned foolishness about rustled beef. But they didn't stop to talk. They come to burn us out . . . and they did it damned quick! Bud Hurley said to pass out the word they'd make the same kind of medicine for anyone else caught with Hurley beef."

Kinsley spoke across the bar with resignation. "There you are, Lucas. It's your baby now. What're you gonna do?"

Wrathful comments, oaths, threats came from the listeners.

Tom raised his voice. "Wait a minute, men! I want to get this straight. Latigo, are you saying they found Hurley beef inside our fences?"

"Claimed they did," snorted Latigo. "It's a damned lie, of course."

"Bound to be." Tom nodded. He was trying to be calm, but the thought of their buildings going up in flames pounded at his brain. "We'll damned quick find out about it."

18

"Sure we will," Latigo promised harshly. "I met Cal Hardesty and a couple others on the road. They're ridin' for help."

"We don't need help. I'll ride to the Double-O and have this out with Bob Hurley."

"Like hell you will, Tom. I'll side you every step. There's others here that'll go, too. Bud Hurley has made killin' talk."

Latigo had his way about it. Eight armed men accompanied Tom out of town. Sheriff Bowlings, uneasy, a bit uncertain, rode with them. They were not heading for a gunfight. Bowlings had made that clear. He wanted facts, nothing else. But the others were grimly ready for anything.

II

The sun was high and hot above a scattered fleece of clouds as the grim knot of riders headed up the trail for the Double-O. Dust drifted lazily about the horses. The heat over the landscape was a brooding heat, like the brooding angel that rode with those homesteaders.

Not a man but knew that this day's happenings could send death racing over the range faster than fire through dry grass. The tinder had been making for years. Bud Hurley had thrown the spark. Only Old Bob could say now what would happen.

Tom Lucas thought of other things, of the years when he had been a Hurley man. Nothing in those years had suggested that his hand would ever lift against the Hurleys. The occasional arrogance of Bud Hurley might have been a warning, Tom knew. But he had always kept the peace with Bud.

There was Marcia. What of Marcia? This was something bigger than friendship. This was Latigo Blair's affair as much as Tom's. This was the concern of all the small ranchers. And, no less, it was the concern of Old Bob Hurley. He wouldn't stop at burning out just one homestead.

They cut the shallow, sandy bends of Brandy Creek and crossed the Arroyo Hondo. The sandstones were yellow and red here, and the water ran cold out of the distant foothills.

They came through the piñon pines into the rolling range west of Arroyo Hondo, where three generations of Hurleys had seen the headquarters log and adobe buildings increase in number since Bob Hurley first built by Brandy Creek.

The homestead troop did not come unnoticed. For the last three miles, dust rose ahead of them as a rider galloped to give warning of their approach. And when their horses splashed the shallow bed of Brandy Creek and swept up the slope toward the massive main house, Old Bob himself was standing on the long portal with a dozen armed men beside him.

20

Tom swung down from the saddle. The others sat their horses.

Old Bob gave no greeting. A head taller than any other man on the porch, Bob Hurley stood straight, fierce, with his head uncovered, his face set coldly. For a moment the only sounds were the hard breathing of the horses, the creak of saddle leather, the scuffle of feet on the ground. . . . The quiet had an ominous, drawn quality.

Bud Hurley was there—slender, straight, darker than Marcia. He was scowling now with an arrogant, sultry watchfulness. But he had evidently had orders. He was in the background. And Tom noticed his holster was empty. Tom stepped to the portal before he spoke

"I reckon you know why I'm here, Hurley."

"You got burnt out this mornin', Lucas."

"Your orders, I suppose?"

Bob Hurley's glance swept the men behind Tom. He eyed Bowlings, the sheriff, without visible recognition.

"The orders don't matter, Lucas. I stand back of anything that my men may do."

Bowlings cleared his throat and looked uncomfortable. "Something went wrong, I guess," he said. "Bud made a mistake, maybe?"

"If I'd been there with Bud, I'd have told him to go ahead."

Latigo Blair showed white teeth in a grin that was almost genially savage under his mustache.

21

"Now would you?" said Latigo. "That's about all we need to know. Bud turned out to be a wolf . . . so you're steppin' out to lead the pack, huh? You said in town this morning it'd be war. You made the first move. By God, now it is war. Come on, men! We wasted time ridin' out here."

Bud Hurley started to speak. Old Bob cut him off with a curt gesture.

"Wait, all of you!" boomed Old Bob. "Since you've come out here, you might as well carry back the truth."

Bob Hurley said something under his breath to Bud, who stalked toward the back of the house.

Latigo's savage grin appeared again. "We got all the truth we need," he snapped. "The old tricks ain't workin' no more. We're callin' your hand this time. And your cards are short as hell for the showdown. Watch it work out."

Old Bob eyed Latigo indifferently. "You men didn't come here for the truth. You came to get Bud. You should've known better. My Double-O brand was here when some of you was guzzlin' pap. It'll stay here if I have to clean out every thievin' nester this side of Sister's Peaks. Bowlings, you're the law. This is for you to judge. But think careful what you do about it."

Three Double-O riders came hazing a yearling around the end of the house. Bud appeared and snaked out a rope and brought the yearling down.

Bob Hurley stalked toward the spot. "Turn him over!" he ordered as the men crowded around, keeping in two bunches. "That's your yearlin', ain't it, Lucas?"

Tom nodded, his eyes narrowing. "That's our Wagon Wheel brand, Colonel."

"It ain't a fresh brand?"

Tom admitted it wasn't.

"How many head of our stock have you got over here?" Latigo growled.

Old Bob ignored the question. "There's more ways to skin a cat than kill him and sharpen a knife. You've all heard of this trick, but nobody was expecting it, I guess. Last year I fixed part of my calf crop with half dollars. The last week or so we've been lookin' for them. Bud found one this mornin'. Bowlings, feel down here."

Bowlings grasped the loose skin low on the yearling's neck. His face changed. He shot a quick frown at Tom, who had stepped to his side.

"I'll be damned," the sheriff muttered.

Silence had fallen. Every eye was on Tom's hand as it felt the same spot. A sick feeling hollowed Tom's middle as he felt the outlines of a half dollar under the loose skin.

"Want it cut out?" Bob Hurley demanded coldly.

Latigo stepped forward truculently. "It's a damned lie!" he cried. "Tom, there ain't a half dollar under that hide, is there?"

Tom gestured helplessly.

Bowling's scowl was mirrored on the faces of the others who had ridden along. They had come, angrily certain they were in the right. Bob Hurley had cut the ground from under them, made them seem ridiculous. More than that, the Double-O had thrown this guilt squarely at all the small ranchers.

Latigo's face was red as he straightened over the yearling. "It's a trick," he gritted. "We ain't branded any maverick this year. Ain't that so, Tom?"

But even Latigo's manner was questioning. And, if the truth were told, Tom had been wondering the same thing about Latigo.

"Well, you two?" Bowlings demanded harshly. "How about it?"

Latigo glared at the sheriff.

Tom spoke to Old Bob Hurley, who was eyeing him like a stranger. He spoke painfully. "That's our brand. Your money's in the hide. I know it ain't a trick of yours. But we don't know how our brand and your silver got together."

Bud Hurley's grunt of derision was audible.

Old Bob wheeled on his grandson. "Damn you, Bud . . . I'll make all the noise here!" Old Bob turned back, bitter with scorn. "Lucas, I was like a father to you when you needed a father. I made you welcome in my house. I helped you get a start on your own land. I've backed you up since you were a kid. And the first chance you get, you turn on me like the dirtiest kind of a nester. You done that to me . . . the one man in the world who'd been your friend!"

White-lipped, Tom said: "You're wrong. I don't expect you to believe it . . . but that's how it is."

"Hell, no, I don't believe you! That half dollar puts the lie in your teeth. You must've been rotten from the start, Lucas. As soon as you got out on your own, you turned greedy, too. Only you're worse than the others. They don't owe me anything. My beef's fair game to them if they're that kind of rascals. But you, Lucas, are a damned ungrateful ingrate. Get off Double-O land and keep off! Bowlings, what I said in town this morning stands. I'll drive every man out of these parts I catch cuttin' in on Double-O beef."

Bob Hurley spat and, with a gesture, added: "Bowlings, here's your chance. Here's a rustlin' charge against these two. What you gonna do about it?"

Jack O'Leary, square-shouldered owner of the Flying M, had come along; he broke his silence truculently. "Not so fast, Hurley. They deny they've throwed a crooked loop. That's good enough for some of us, this far. Time enough to arrest 'em when someone else finds your half dollars."

The other men promptly backed up O'Leary.

Bowlings shrugged uncomfortably. "Something

to that," he said. "Maybe we've all been a little hasty. I'll think it over. Lucas and Blair'll be around if I want them."

Bob Hurley lost his temper. "I figured it'd turn out this way. Get goin' off Double-O land. And from today on, my fences are a deadline for any man who doesn't draw Hurley pay or hasn't got business here at the house. Spread the word, you men! Guns'll back it up!"

Old Bob threw the last over his shoulder as he stamped toward the house. His men straggled watchfully after him.

Tom had to spur to keep up with the others as they galloped away from that scene of ignominious failure. Not until they were miles away from the house, trotting the winded horses, did Jack O'Leary call over unpleasantly: "Lucas, you sure made a hell of a mess of that. What was the idea of acting so damned high and mighty if there was any chance old Hurley could pin something on you? You might've known he had aces up his sleeve when he burned you out."

"Got your mind made up we're guilty, I see," replied Tom shortly.

"You're guilty as hell, as far as I'm concerned," said O'Leary. "He had you both cold. I horned in because I didn't want to see him taking the whole deal. He'd have had Bowlings slap handcuffs on you next."

"I ain't sure yet it wasn't a trick," put in Bowlings defensively. "If I was sure Lucas and Blair rustled that yearling, I'd put them under arrest."

O'Leary sneered. "You better hunker down and make sure who's right in this. Hurley didn't elect you. Hurley ain't the man who'll elect you again. Think it over. There's a heap of us has got a stake in this."

Bowlings shrugged and made no reply. But every man knew Bowlings would stretch points from hell to leather to make sure he was on the winning side.

Tom and Latigo turned off shortly after that to cut across country toward their ranch.

Bowlings seemed glad to be rid of them. But he clung to his dignity with a last warning: "Don't leave these parts without coming to me first."

Latigo snorted: "Who in hell wants to leave? We've still got a ranch. We'll be on it when Hurley is forgot around here."

Latigo rode in morose silence for half a mile before he spoke again.

"Tom, we're partners. One of us makes a mistake, we both take it. Man to man, do you know anything about that damned yearlin'?"

"No savvy," said Tom. He grinned wryly. "We're both scratching dirt and eyeing one another. Man to man, Latigo, how about you?"

"No savvy, either," swore Latigo, and he, too,

27

grinned crookedly. "Now that's settled, how in hell did that half dollar and our brand get together?"

Tom shook his head. "Right now, all I can do is wonder what'll come out of it."

"Plenty, I guess," decided Latigo. "Meanwhile, we're burned out and branded cow thieves. What do we do?"

"Find out how much more Hurley silver we're pasturing," Tom said. His jaw hardened. "And then look around and find out how come."

Two hands were all they hired—Johnny Waite, bowlegged, pint-sized, white-haired range veteran, and young Pete Salazar, half Yaqui, half Mexican from the Sonora cattle country.

Pete Salazar had been at the house with Latigo when the Hurley men stormed up. Johnny Waite was there when Tom and Latigo rode in. Johnny was still sulphurous every time he squinted at the smoldering ruins of the house.

"Burnt up my whiskey bottle, my pipe, boxes of cartridges, and my fiddle," Johnny snarled, bowlegging back and forth by the windmill trough, where Latigo and Tom had dismounted. "What in hell are we comin' to when a low-down bunch of range snakes can come in and do this?"

Tom chuckled. "Your pipe smelled terrible, Johnny, and that rotgut whiskey only made you play that squeaky fiddle more off tune."

Pete Salazar pointed to a square of canvas on the ground. Piled on the canvas were a charred side of bacon, some fire-blackened canned goods that had not burst, a water bucket full of dirty flour, flame-scarred kitchenware, their bedrolls, and three sacks of smoking tobacco.

"*Poco bueno*," Pete said, grinning. "Plenty grub, and the ground she's dry."

"That's a Mex for you," snorted Johnny Waite. "When I come back, he was full of beans and bacon, hunkered down, cat-nappin', with a cigarette burnin' his lip."

"Well, she's all burn' down, so what I do alone?" countered Pete comfortably.

Tom looked up at the sun. "How about some canned beans, Pete? I see Johnny ain't hungry, but Latigo and I can eat the cans, too."

"Who said I wasn't hungry?" growled Johnny. "But, hell's fire, ain't we goin' to make some trouble for those damned raiders?"

"Take your time about eatin'," advised Latigo grimly. "Chances are you'll get your hell soon enough."

Grub lifted their spirits. Tom rolled a cigarette, stared impassively at the ruins.

"We'll build up again," he said. "Bud Hurley didn't burn the grass or take the beef. Pete, ride into town for some more grub. The buckboard's at the livery barn with the other horse. Bring back a couple of tents."

"And some cartridges," reminded Johnny stiffly.

"Saddle trouble," Tom grinned, "is all you'll have for a few days, Johnny. We'll scout our yearlings and see how many of them really belong to our own cows."

Pete Salazar headed out. Tom, Latigo, and Johnny Waite were saddling when Latigo stared past the corral and dryly commented: "Tom, I reckon this is your hand to play."

A woman was riding toward them. And Tom's heart was pounding as he rode out to meet her—to meet Marcia Hurley.

III

Marcia was on King, her own long-legged bay gelding. She was wearing small, gaily stitched riding boots, a divided skirt, a jaunty sombrero. With a braided quirt hanging from her gloved wrist, a bright silk handkerchief fluttering at her neck, she once more looked like a ranch girl.

Marcia's face, as they met, was pale and troubled. "Hello, Tom," she said quietly.

"Hello, Marcia."

Awkward silence fell on them. Their horses moved restlessly. Marcia's bay breathed hard from its run.

"You didn't do it, Tom?"

"What do you think, Marcia?"

She drew a long breath and looked away. "Of course, you didn't. But they think you did. This . . . this isn't the end of it."

"How so?"

"They'll keep after you until you leave."

Tom smiled thinly. "That's what they think."

The girl nodded, troubled. "Of course, they won't. But . . . but you know how stubborn grandfather can be. And Bud is hot-headed . . ."

"And spoiling for trouble," Tom finished for her.

"I'm afraid so," Marcia said miserably. "That's why I had to see you, Tom. You're the only one who'll listen to me. This can't go on until someone is killed. If you'd tell me, you won't let anything happen . . ."

"How, Marcia?"

She gestured helplessly. "I don't know. If you . . . or your men . . . don't shoot first . . ."

"Just take everything that's thrown at us . . . and not fight back?"

"If it were only someone else!" Marcia cried wretchedly. She had to swallow a lump in her throat. "Tom, no matter who else is hurt in this, I'll be hurt. Doesn't that mean anything?"

"If I was hurt, how much would it mean?" Tom asked.

Color came to Marcia's face. She looked away.

"How much do you think, Tom? How . . . how blind are you?"

"Stone blind and afraid to think," Tom said huskily.

He edged his horse close and put out an arm. And Marcia leaned to meet him. Moments later she was laughing unsteadily as she pushed him away.

"Tom, the men at the windmill are enjoying this."

"Let them," said Tom.

"Yes, I know. You *are* an idiot, Tom. You should have known a long time ago. But now everything's all right. . . . Isn't it? Nothing can happen now, Tom?"

"I'll keep the peace somehow . . . keep it if it kills me," Tom promised. "Come on. I'll ride toward home with you. It's too crowded around here."

Halfway to the Hurley fences, Tom turned back, circling out on his own land to look for yearlings. He was singing when he rode over the lip of a draw and found Latigo and Johnny Waite just releasing a yearling, which bolted off indignantly as Tom rode up.

Latigo's look was enigmatic. "Feeling your oats, I see," he commented.

"Why not?" Tom grinned, unabashed. "I've got everything now I ever wanted."

"You've got a hell of a lot more trouble to handle," Latigo said cynically. "Uhn-huh. It just about needed somethin' like this to finish the day up right. Wait'll Old Man Hurley finds out. He'll bust a gall bladder. But jawin' about it won't help," Latigo relented. "She's a fine girl, Tom. I'm for you both. And we ain't found any half dollars so far."

"Scatter out and keep looking."

They straggled in to the windmill before dark. Latigo, who had come back first, had a fire going. There was grub enough for another meal. Later, they were sitting around the blazing fire when the pound of hoofs became audible off in the night. All three backed into the darkness, with their guns ready.

But the riders were not Hurley men.

Cal Hardesty, of the N-Cross-N, led them— thirteen men in all, armed to the teeth. And Cal Hardesty came to the point as they crowded around the campfire.

"We figured to lift some Hurley hair tonight. Thought you'd like to be in on it, Lucas. The Hurleys'll be too damned cocky, now that they've caught you cold."

"Think we're guilty, Hardesty?"

"Hell, yes! But that ain't the point. Who's runnin' this range is the point."

"Maybe," said Tom, "but we aren't interested in proving it."

Hardesty stared. "Has Hurley got you bluffed?"

"We're not looking for trouble," Tom repeated.

"How about you, Latigo?" Hardesty asked.

"Tom's makin' the deal," Latigo retorted glumly.

"Plain enough, I guess," Cal Hardesty sneered. "Come on, boys. We've got business to do."

"Wait a minute," Tom said. "Stay off Hurley land tonight. We'll get the blame for anything you do."

"Are you givin' us orders, Lucas?"

"I'm telling you, Hardesty. Make a mess of trouble for us tonight, and I'll come looking for you."

Cal Hardesty seethed for a moment. His gun arm was tense as he stood, spread-legged, glaring across the fire.

Latigo drawled: "Feelin' reckless tonight, Cal?"

"All right," Hardesty decided abruptly. "I'll stay off as a favor to you . . . nothin' else. Let's get back to town, men."

Latigo cursed under his breath as they rode away. "First we're cow thieves. Now they figure we're yellow. God knows what we'll be by tomorrow night!"

The next day Latigo found a Wagon Wheel yearling that had a Hurley half dollar under its hide. Latigo fired a shot that brought Tom.

"This makes two. There's probably more,"

Tom said soberly. "I'll take this critter over to the Double-O. Maybe Bob Hurley'll see reason today and help us find the son who did it."

"You're a glutton for trouble," Latigo said resignedly. "We'll both go."

Tom shook his head. "Your temper's too flashy. I'll handle it alone this time. Nobody'll shoot me in the back."

"You're a damned idiot," Latigo said bluntly. "But have your own way. There's such a thing as fool's luck."

It was a two-hour trip to the Hurley fence line. Tom cut the Hurley road halfway there, and not far along lost his grim mood when Marcia met him.

"Good thing you rode out this way!" Tom called as Marcia drew near. "I was getting mighty hungry to see you. Still love me, Miss Hurley?"

"I'll not be questioned," Marcia said, pink-cheeked and laughing. "And I wasn't hunting you. Do you usually take a yearling along when you ride out to see a lady?"

Tom sobered. "We found another one. I'm taking him to your grandfather. I want to talk this thing over with him."

"No, Tom . . . No! Don't try it. Anyway, grandfather rode into town this morning. I'm going in to meet him. Tom, *please* don't go inside our fence. You might meet Bud. And you know Bud. He'll make trouble."

"You're the boss. Maybe I'll come on into town after you. Ask your grandfather if he'll talk to me there."

"I'll try," Marcia promised doubtfully.

Tom caught a glimpse of a single rider, far back, when he looked around unexpectedly. He rode over the next rise of ground, turned to the right for a short distance, then stopped behind a screening juniper to watch his back trail.

The rider was Johnny Waite. He looked sheepish when Tom galloped out and met him.

"Latigo said I'd better follow you . . . just in case," said Johnny.

"Latigo's worse than an old woman. But you might as well come along now," Tom said. "I'm going on into town."

They ran the yearling inside the Hurley gate. Johnny was fastening the gate when two riders came galloping up. Bud Hurley was one, and he was angry, challenging.

"What are you up to now, Lucas?"

"I brought another one of your half dollars back. I'd like to talk to you about it, Bud. There's something wrong here."

"You're damned right there's something wrong," was Bud's ugly reply. "Your thieving heart is what's wrong." Bud carried a rifle. He lifted it now in a threatening gesture. "You had your orders. Get caught inside this fence, and you get this." Bud jerked his head at the hard-faced rider with him, who packed two guns and a rifle. "Every man on the place has his orders."

Bud's companion showed even teeth under a black mustache. Short, heavy-set, heavy-browed, his looks were not helped by a broken nose.

"First one of you inside the wire gets dropped like a rabbit," he said genially.

Johnny Waite's smoldering fury burst out. "Watch you don't get the same thing when you step outside the wire. There's two ways of playin' that game."

"Shut up, Johnny," Tom ordered, reining around and riding off.

"That's Old Man Hurley for you!" Johnny fumed as he followed. "Bringin' in gunmen like that to keep the pan sizzlin'."

"Ever see the fellow before?"

"Never did."

"Funny about him," mused Tom. "He looks more than a run-of-the-chute gunfighter. Hurley is hiring some mighty hard-looking *hombres*. This fellow was walking around yesterday at the house like he was giving orders next to Old Bob himself."

"Wouldn't put it past the old wolf to hire him an outlaw bunch," said Johnny peevishly.

"If he does, he may get burnt with his own fire."

Tom's thoughts went to Marcia as they rode on into town. She would be the one to suffer if any more serious trouble broke out. And yet what could be done? Trouble was rolling before the wind like tumbleweeds piling in a fence corner. . . . But a man can't see the wind, can't draw a bead on it.

In town, Johnny Waite cut off alone to have a splinter of a time. And Tom found other things to think about.

More than one man gave him a knowing grin. There were others who scowled at him, and some who drifted hastily into doorways or cut across the street to avoid meeting him.

Pete Salazar hadn't mentioned this. The town was taking sides. Some didn't care if he and Latigo had rustled Hurley beef. Some did. But no one seemed to doubt that they had done it.

Tom looked for Marcia. Instead, he found Old Bob Hurley coming out of the hardware store with Concho Stevans, another old-timer.

Tom stopped them. "I've something to talk over with you, Hurley. I'd consider it a favor if you'd listen to me."

Old Bob gave him a burning look. His voice had the same implacable harshness. "Marcia said she met you with another one of my yearlin's. I ain't surprised, Lucas. I had my say yesterday. I don't want any truck with you. I'll settle with you in my own way and time."

Tom started to say something, but Old Bob brushed past him and walked on, growling something to Concho Stevans. Men on both sides of the street had seen the meeting. Several within sight were grinning.

Tom swore under his breath as he turned on his heel and walked the other way. You couldn't do anything with a man like Bob Hurley, proddy, ready to reach for his gun the instant his fierce convictions were inflamed. Tom knew when he was whipped. He'd never be able to pull a gun on Marcia's grandfather, no matter what happened. He'd never be able to edge into a fight with a man who'd done for him what Old Bob Hurley had done in years past. Hurley had damned him over the length and breadth of the home range—and there was nothing he could do about it in return. . . . Tom turned into the nearest saloon and bought a drink.

Half an hour later, at the back end of the bar, he was moody, with four drinks under his belt and another between his fingers. Tom knew he was a fool. This wasn't the time to be drinking. He needed a steady head to think. Better look up Marcia—but that would make a brush with Old Bob. The thing to do was to get back to the ranch and figure about those Hurley half dollars. There didn't seem to be much chance to find out anything in town.

"How about settin' in on some draw, Lucas?" someone called to him from a table over along the wall.

Tom knew the three men who were sitting down to play. They were friends; probably they were going out of their way to show it.

He shook his head. "No, I guess not this time."

"Come on, Tom," Charley Raymond said. "Maybe this is your lucky day. We need another hand."

"I'll sit in for an hour," Tom decided.

He started to the table—and stopped short. Gunfire had burst out down the street!

Charley Raymond kicked back his chair and followed Tom's rush to the door. The others were close behind.

"Sounds like some outfit shooting up the town," Charley Raymond yelled as he ran out the door.

Tom didn't think that. In his black mood, he expected trouble. This was a gunfight, not the exuberant slap and slam of reckless shots.

One look through the hot, bright sunshine flooding the dusty street was enough to give him the vivid picture. Men were boiling out of Dick Kinsley's Shorthorn Saloon, across the street. Horses were plunging at the hitch rack as guns blasted in their faces.

And a rider who had run out, shooting, was in the saddle now, yanking his horse around and spurring down the street. Squinting in the bright sunlight, Tom didn't recognize the horse. But the man's back, as dust flew from the driving hoofs, was recognizable. Johnny Waite! It was bowlegged little Johnny Waite, riding for his life.

A man who Tom had seen only twice, but knew instantly, ran out into the open and lifted a rifle. It was the gaudily dressed gunman who had been riding the Hurley fence line with Bud Hurley. Tom stopped short.

IV

Tom's six-shooter whipped out of its holster. The distance was too great for a handgun to do much. But there wasn't any other hope for Johnny—not with that rifle leveling at such close range. Tom found his target in the sights for a rigid instant, and gently squeezed the trigger.

But it was a lost hope; he had that dread feeling as the weapon recoiled in his hand. The rifle spat sharply half a breath later. Its steadiness had not been changed.

Johnny rode on for half a dozen strides. Then, without struggling, he slid forward and off one side of the saddle. His foot twisted in the stirrup and locked there. Johnny's head and shoulders bounced and flopped and dragged horribly in a yellow cloud of dust as the horse plunged on.

The crowd that had boiled out of the saloons and stores ran after the horse. Down the street beyond the horse, several men ran out waving their arms to stop the bolting animal. Tom was half sobbing in blind fury as he ran, gun cocked and ready, his eyes on the running back of the man who had killed Johnny. Johnny had been a loyal little cuss. There was no doubt that he was dead. You had the feeling as he slid out of the saddle that life was already gone from him.

The horse veered over to the left, plunged, bucked. The stirrup strap broke, and what was left of Johnny subsided in the dirt. Everybody was running to the spot. Tom doubted that any of them had heard his shot. He could see the tall figure of Old Bob Hurley with the sheriff, the sheriff's deputy, and one or two other Hurley men. It looked as though they had jumped Johnny in a bunch.

But there was one man who wasn't following. He came around the Shorthorn hitch rack and cut across the street to intercept Tom.

"Wait a minute, Lucas." It was Cal Hardesty.

Tom panted his reply without stopping: "Don't bother me, damn you."

Cal Hardesty ran in as Tom passed, caught his arm, and swung him around.

"Don't go there, Lucas. They'll kill you. You're next. Hear me? You're next!"

"Me next?" Tom panted angrily. "What do you mean? If you're trying to keep me away from those murdering sons who cut down Johnny just then . . ."

"Hold your horses," snapped Hardesty. He was

breathing hard from his dash across the street. His manner had an urgency that carried its own conviction of truth. "Bud Hurley has been shot . . . plugged in the back while he was ridin' the Hurley fence line. Does that mean anything to you?"

"Hell, no! Why should it?" But Tom felt his middle hollowing out.

"The blame has been laid on you and Johnny Waite."

"It's a damned lie!" Tom rasped with a sudden rush of fury.

"That ain't helpin' you any. It didn't help Johnny Waite just then. Old Man Hurley's like a crazy man. Get outta town quick before they spot you. Cut around to my ranch and wait there for me. God knows where else you'll be safe, unless you ride off of this range for good."

Cal Hardesty had swung Tom around, was urging him toward the saloon doorway. "Run out the back way, Lucas. Get off the street. I'll bring your horse around. Where is it?"

"Up the street there, a couple doors down," Tom said harshly. "I'll get it myself. I'll not take cover like a rabbit from something I'm not guilty of."

"You're a fool, Lucas."

And the next minute Tom knew he probably was a fool, under the circumstances, for he heard a bellow from the spot where Johnny had fallen.

Old Bob Hurley's voice rang over all other sounds. "There's the other one! Get him!"

Tom ran then, ran for his life, as Hardesty ducked into the nearest doorway. Guns began to blast. There would be no chance to argue, to explain. Old Bob Hurley didn't want explanations now. A dead man was the only thing his raging grief would have.

The crowd was in the street. Briefly, Tom had the cover of horses and buggies at the hitch racks along the walk. His horse stamped back as Tom ducked under the hitch bar, flipped the reins off, threw himself into the saddle. Spurs and a yank on the reins spun the horse around the end of the hitch rack, along the sidewalk. In the open street, horse and rider would be a perfect target—as Johnny Waite had been. On the walk, there was some protection.

A man hurried out of a doorway, gave one startled look at the bolting horse bearing down on him, and scrambled back.

The shots were blasting faster, coming high and wild. Tom saw brick dust spurt from a building front ahead. He heard a pane of glass break as he passed. He felt a bullet drill through his hat. . . .

The one vacant lot on this side of the street loomed up ahead. Tom plunged his horse into it. He was safe for a moment. He turned into the alley at the back, turned again at the cross street, made another turn at the next corner over. . . .

And he had the start that was his only chance.

The home ranch was to the north. Latigo and Pete Salazar were there. They'd throw in their guns. But at the ranch there were not even buildings in which to hole up and fight. Riding there would be like bringing death to two men who hadn't earned it.

Tom rode east. His galloping horse swept under the leafy cottonwoods at the edge of town. Mexican men, women, and children stared as he raced past their reddish adobe huts. Mongrel dogs ran out to bark—and skulked back, as if sensing that hell had taken this road for the moment.

Looking over his shoulder, Tom saw the first of the pursuit stringing out well behind. They were not wasting shots. They were riding to close in and make certain of the kill.

Beyond town the road swung northeast toward the Concho River, miles away. Tom headed up a sandy, winding draw, and rode toward the dry San Martin brakes.

The going was bad, trails were few this way. For fifteen miles, a man would find no moisture but the sweat from his parching body. But the country was broken, and most of the time a man could keep screened from guns not too close behind. And if he had to turn and fight, he could find a cutbank, a screen of rocks, some cover, to make his stand.

The pace was torture for a horse. Pursuers who

rode to kill and a fugitive who rode to live, could spare no sympathy for horseflesh.

As he rode out of that first draw, Tom realized he had to lose those guns behind. For as he came over the rise, he showed plainly against the deep blue of the sky.

A bullet tore the flesh of his right arm, up near the shoulder. A whip might have lashed the spot. The brief shock left the arm slightly numb. Looking down, Tom saw the bullet tear in the coat sleeve. But he could use the arm. He could ride. He spurred hard down the opposite slope, cut past the end of a small hill, and had cover again.

The grass had thinned to scanty tufts. Cactus, greasewood, and water-scoured slopes cut by parched draws and arroyos made up the landscape as far as he could see. The heat hung low in quivering sheets.

No horse could stand this pace for long. From the next rise, Tom looked back to the yellow dust hanging above the first riders. He was pulling ahead. He eased the pace, held his lead, and came safely to the Arroyo Hondo.

Steep and eroded, the arroyo banks sided a channel some four hundred yards wide. In flood, once or twice a year, it ran water. But now white sand and water-worn rocks, *chamiso* thickets, and little clay islands between the arroyo channels lay dusty and dry under the searing sun.

Foam spotted the horse's neck as it crossed the arroyo and took the other side. Tom reined in and leaped from the saddle. His face was grim. He'd be afoot if the horse was punished much more.

In a depression beyond the arroyo bank, he dismounted, wrapped the reins low around the pole-like branches of an ocotillo cactus, jerked his rifle from the saddle, and ran back to the arroyo bank.

The arm was hurting. Blood streaked his wrist and hand. Tom wiped the hand against his leg, as he dropped behind two rocks that were partly screened by a *chamiso* bush. He levered a cartridge into the chamber. He could hear his horse blowing through flaring nostrils. High overhead a buzzard lazily circled. Tom grinned coldly at the omen.

Then the first rider appeared on the opposite bank, scanned the arroyo for a moment, and rode down to cross. Others followed. Four . . . five riders were sweeping across that open channel.

Tom tested the wind, set his sights, held his aim long and carefully on the first horse. His trigger squeeze was gentle. He was not surprised to see the horse stumble and drop, the rider corkscrewing down in an ugly fall. The man rolled over and got up, limping.

The other riders stopped. Nearby *chamiso* offered the men cover, but not the horses.

The animals milled in indecision. Again Tom squeezed the trigger, and again a horse went down.

The three who were left retreated at a gallop. Others who had appeared on the bank waited there. The two dismounted men had vanished in the dusty *chamiso*. Tom let them go. He did not want to kill a man.

He reached his horse without showing himself and rode off easily. The pursuit was stopped for a time.

V

Two hours before midnight, Tom rode the jaded horse into Cal Hardesty's N-Cross-N, to the south. Lights were burning in the ranch house. Pete Salazar's voice hailed him out of the darkness.

"Yeah, it's me, Pete!" called Tom with relief. It was good to hear his own man; he hadn't expected this.

Pete Salazar had a rifle. He took the reins as Tom wearily dismounted. A house door had opened. Men were coming out.

Pete Salazar said: "*Por Dios*, ees good to see you, *señor*. That posse bring back word ees blood at El Hondo. 'So what?' we say. *Señor* Latigo ees like one wild man."

"Tom?" That was Latigo now, hurrying up. And Cal Hardesty followed.

It was good to give Pete the horse, to walk stiffly into the lighted house, to down the big drink Cal Hardesty poured before he asked a question. The whiskey burned hot and strong inside. Tom's dusty face grinned wryly.

"Get this arm bandaged, and I'll be fit as a fiddle. Latigo, how come you and Pete are here?"

"Hardesty sent a man for us," replied Latigo. "Said you were makin' a ride for it, and chances were you'd show up here sooner or later if you got away. Wasn't nothin' we could do to help you, so we came here, hopin' for the best."

"I stopped them at the Hondo. They didn't sight me after that." Tom's face darkened as he spoke. "What about Bud Hurley?"

Latigo cursed under his breath for a moment. "Bud's plenty dead. And it's laid onto you and Johnny Waite."

"Who laid it?"

"Fellow ridin' with Bud . . . one of Hurley's new men," Latigo said.

Hardesty said: "His name's Larsen. He's there on the Hurley place with a bunch of his own men."

"Gunslingers?"

"What else? Seems he and Bud was ridin' fence and caught you and Waite tryin' to shove another of them buzzard yearlings back. There

49

were words. You threatened to kill Bud, and they got the drop on you and Waite, and then ran you both off. And a little later, along the fence, Bud was bushwhacked, and Larsen got a bullet through his hat. I saw the hole. Larsen says he turned to fight, but Bud was dead and there was nothin' to get his gun on. But there wasn't any doubt who did it. Old Bob didn't take breath before he called for a killin'. They found Waite first."

Tom's bloodshot, dust-rimmed eyes met Hardesty's thin, cold smile and Latigo's bushy-browed scowl.

"There's just enough truth there to damn Johnny and me," Tom said heavily.

"You did a good thing, a heap of us feel," said Hardesty. "Bud was askin' for trouble."

"Kinda figure I did it, eh?"

"It doesn't matter to me," disclaimed Hardesty.

"I've been wondering why you ran across the street to warn me and said to hole up here. You'd rather gut shoot me, Hardesty . . . and maybe I've felt the same about you."

Hardesty shrugged. "Gut shootin' each other doesn't do anything about the Hurleys. The small outfits have to stick together. Old Man Hurley has run a hot iron on you twice now. If I add it up right, you're gettin' to the point where you'll lead a roundup against him. Everybody's seen what's happened to you. A lot of men'll ride with you a damned sight quicker than they will with anyone else."

"I figured you had an iron in the fire," Tom said. "But this range isn't all skunk. A heap of men that hate Bob Hurley would refuse to ride with an *hombre* that had bushwhacked Bud."

"Maybe you didn't do it," Hardesty said with a faint sneer.

"You're askin' for trouble doubtin' it!" gritted Latigo. "I know Tom. He wouldn't have killed Bud face to face . . . let alone cuttin' him down from behind."

"It'll be hard to prove," Hardesty said, with another of his thin, cold smiles. "Lucas is due for a skinful of lead from the Hurleys, or a rope from the law, unless . . ."

"Unless what?" challenged Tom.

Hardesty shrugged. "Unless Old Hurley is cut down to where he doesn't count anymore. Then it won't matter a damn what you did."

Narrow-eyed, Tom considered Hardesty's words. "With Bud just dead, and posses looking for me, this isn't the time for me to go after Bob Hurley."

"Take it easy here until the time comes."

"I can't do much else," Tom decided.

Tom avoided the disgusted look under Latigo's bushy brows. "I'll go see about my horse, and then grub a little and sleep. Come on, Latigo, I want to know what you aim to do."

Outside in the night, Latigo was scathing. "Tom, are you gonna hole up here like a cornered range rat and play Hardesty's game?"

"Since when did you start backing Bob Hurley, Latigo?"

"I ain't started. But Hardesty is usin' you to pull his meat out of the fire. Hell, Tom, it ain't like you. Why not try to find out who killed Bud? Why not face Bob Hurley and have it out man to man, with me backin' you up? I don't like this stringin' with Hardesty."

Tom was silent for a moment, then bleak, as he spoke: "There isn't anyone else to string with, Latigo. I need time to think. Cal Hardesty'll make damned sure no one finds me here."

"I don't like it, Tom."

"Your neck's safe, Latigo. Cut loose from me and do what you're minded to."

"You'll rile me in a minute, Tom. When I cut loose from a pardner, it won't be when he's in trouble."

"You're stubborn and pig-headed, Latigo. And you're a crazy fool to mix in this anymore."

"That ain't even an argument," snorted Latigo. "I'll head back to town tonight."

Pete Salazar had his own ideas. "So moch funny beesness," he said a little later, with his brown face impassive. "I think I look around for two, three days, no?"

"Go ahead," said Tom.

Hardesty rode into town the next day. He was back at dusk.

"They figure you kept goin'," Hardesty said, with satisfaction.

"What's Bob Hurley doing?" Tom asked.

"He was in town buyin' a coffin. I saw him across the street. His face looked kind of frozen. Never saw him look quite like it. He's showin' his age. My bet is he's gettin' ready to fold up and quit. He aimed to have Bud take over the ranch one of these days, you know. With Bud gone, there ain't much reason to keep on."

"Bud has a sister."

Hardesty shrugged. "A woman don't count. She'll be glad to get back East."

Tom fought down a desire to reach out and smash Hardesty's thin face, with its cold, greenish eyes.

"You don't know Old Bob," he said shortly, and walked off.

Latigo returned the next morning.

While he was unsaddling out at the horse corral, he talked to Tom.

"Funeral's today, at the ranch," he said jerkily, swearing as he strained his wounded arm. "Two good arms left between us . . . which makes us just about one he-man."

"One he-man can kick up plenty of dust, Latigo.

53

Did you hear anything about this man Larsen?"

"Nary a word."

"I've been thinking about Larsen," Tom said, squinting against the sun.

"He's a hardcase."

"They can be softened up. If somebody wanted Bud's killing laid on me, it couldn't have been pulled off better."

"I reckon that's so."

"Nobody knew I'd be there at the Hurley fence, let alone be there at the time Bud came along. It couldn't have been planned."

Latigo heaved his saddle to the ground and nodded.

Tom went on, with a wiry quality in his voice. "Larsen lied about his side of it. I never threatened to kill Bud. Nobody got the drop on us. I shut Johnny up and rode away. Larsen lied like hell. He must know how Bud died. If he lied about Johnny and me, chances are he lied about how Bud died."

"Why didn't you say that the other night?" Latigo's mouth was hard under his drooping mustache. His gaunt figure had straightened with attention.

"Wanted to think it over and let the dust settle. This isn't the time to be making mistakes."

"I'll get that dirty wolf and shove a six-gun down his guzzle. I'll get the truth out of him, if I have to blast it out."

"That isn't the answer. I'd do it myself, but Bob Hurley wouldn't believe it." Tom stared past the corral to the cottonwoods beyond the house. "If Bob Hurley doesn't believe it, Latigo, the truth isn't much good. I've got a headache from trying to get around that. I don't know what's to be done."

"Do you think Larsen killed Bud?"

Tom nodded. "Larsen was there with Bud. Larsen was the only one who knew I was around. Larsen twisted the facts until they fitted. Hell, *he* must've killed Bud."

"He was workin' for Bud, you might say. What'd Larsen get out of a wolf's trick like that? Next thing you'll be sayin' Larsen salted them yearlin's on us."

Tom shook his head.

"Larsen hasn't been around long enough. What good would it do him, anyway? He couldn't cash in on a trick like that. Somebody else'll do the cashing . . . and Larsen'll get his cut."

"I don't see it," Latigo confessed. "Where's the chips in this game? Somebody want to run you and me off this range? Them salted yearlin's look like it. But killin' Bud Hurley is a hell of a way to go about it."

"I've thought of that," said Tom. "Somebody wanted Bud dead, no matter who got blamed for it. Laying it on me made the pot sweeter. We need a good tracker, Latigo."

"Pete Salazar?"

"I was thinking of him. Pete's all Yaqui on a trail. Put him on Larsen's tracks. You can never tell. That skunk Larsen might nose around some spot he isn't supposed to be."

Latigo's eyes were frosty with purpose as he started to remount. "If I can't find Pete," he promised, "I'll turn Yaqui myself and do it."

VI

They buried Bud Hurley on the home ranch, on the land that Bud one day would have shared with Marcia. Latigo brought Tom Lucas an account of the scene. Old Bob had watched with a stony face, the hope of his old age seeming to vanish into the grave. And not one, but twenty who were there, told of the flitting smile, cold with purpose, that had been on Old Bob's face as he turned away with Marcia, grieving and silent behind her black veil.

"Larsen was there," said Latigo. "Pete's gonna cotton onto him."

"So Bob smiled?" Tom said bleakly. "Latigo, hell is on its way. Rustlers and cows won't count. Bob'll go after the small outfits he figured started this . . . and killed Bud. It's Bob Hurley's last fight, Latigo. And it'll be a good one."

• • •

Hand bills went up for a hundred miles around. The reward for Tom Lucas, five thousand dollars. Five thousand for the man who had killed Bud Hurley. And the range telegraph flashed word that heavily armed strangers were trickling in to the Hurley Ranch. Bob Hurley was hiring more gunmen. Tension mounted among the small outfits.

Gunmen struck the T Cross first, burning buildings, haystacks, ripping down wire that barred Hurley cattle from water and grass the T Cross had fenced off four years back.

The next afternoon riders began to gather at Hardesty's ranch. Tom faced friends, neighbors, for the first time since Bud had died. He found himself popular with most of them. Bud Hurley's death had been a blow at Bob Hurley—and that was all that counted now.

Out by the corrals, where the horses were being fed and watered, Tom spoke bluntly to the gathering men.

"Guns aren't the way. I didn't kill Bud Hurley. I didn't mess with Hurley's beef. You men figure you're right. Bob Hurley is damned sure he's right. And half the good men on this range will be cut down to prove it."

"Who," yelled Cal Hardesty, "gives a damn who did what? Soft words and yellow talk don't help! Guns and lead are all that old wolf'll listen to! If you're yellow, get the hell out of here! Or give yourself up to the sheriff! If you ain't yellow, ride with us! What's it gonna be?"

"Not yellow, you loud-mouthed trouble-hunter!" Tom ripped out. "I'm riding with the rest of you, against those hired gunmen. But not against Bob Hurley."

They rode after dark—thirty-eight nesters, small ranch owners and hands. They cut across the range toward Hurley land. The drum of hoofs on the dry ground rolled threateningly against the night. . . . Tom wondered how dangerous they really were. Some of the nesters were a scrawny lot, boasters, glib talkers, green at this savage game.

Late that evening they cut wire on Hurley's southeast boundary and left it down. They were a mile in Hurley land when a rider on a lathered horse overhauled them.

"The Hurleys are out again tonight, headin' south toward Jim Watson's ranch."

Jim Watson was present. "Maybe there's time to catch 'em!" he cried excitedly. "If we don't, I'll be cleaned out. Damn Bob Hurley's black heart!"

Cal Hardesty objected. "Now's the time to burn out Hurley. His men are away."

"You started after Hurley's gunmen," Tom put in harshly. "Now that you know where they are, go after them."

"You're damned anxious to save Bob Hurley's place, Lucas. We'll get those men later."

Hardesty had little trouble in swinging the men to his way of thinking. Tom thought disgustedly that some of them were spurred on by the knowledge that they could get their revenge now without fighting Hurley's men.

Then Tom was riding south, with Jim Watson, Latigo, and four others—seven men who refused to attack a defenseless ranch at a time when one of their number was being threatened.

They were two miles from Jim Watson's place when the first haystack mushroomed flame and sparks against the night sky. Riding furiously, they heard the first gunshots, and then sighted the house in the red glare of the fire. The house was not yet burning. Jim Watson's seventeen-year-old son, his wife, and one rheumatic hired hand were inside—and they were making a last, brave stand to save the house.

Two haystacks and the bunkhouse were blazing. Well back from the lurid light, shadowy riders were directing a ragged scatter of gunfire at the house.

Tom and the other six raced in with six-guns roaring. Tom's plunging horse bolted through a tangle of juniper. A startled rider tried to wheel away. Tom shot him out of the saddle. He wheeled right, to face another rider who had pulled up short at sight of him.

Tom spurred toward the man. He had the advantage of the light, the red glare silhouetting the rider. He saw a handgun licking flame toward him. His right arm was almost useless, but his left hand was throwing lead. A bullet clubbed his leg and knocked him askew in the saddle. Sick with the shock of it, Tom grabbed the horn to steady himself, and kept on. And the dark figure fled off among the junipers.

That was the story of the fight: a flurry of gunshots, rapid retreat. The man Tom had shot from the saddle was dead. Aside from the burned bunkhouse and haystacks, Jim Watson hadn't suffered much damage.

Latigo was profane as he helped fix Tom's leg. "You've lost a bucket of blood this time," he snorted. "Here's where you squat and keep outta trouble. I reckon Watson won't mind you campin' with him."

"Tom's got a bed here until the cows get gray," Jim Watson said. "There won't be much more trouble, if seven of us cleaned 'em so easy."

"Too damned easy," said Tom shortly. "They ran like they had their orders. Bob Harley wouldn't run that way. I don't like it."

"I'll mosey back the way we come and see what luck Hardesty's had," decided Latigo.

Latigo was back before dawn. His face was long. "You were right, Tom," he said at the bedside.

"Bob Hurley the fox. Most of his men was waitin' at home. Hardesty's bunch was cleaned out, licked so hard they ain't stopped runnin' yet."

"And now Bob Hurley can claim he's protecting himself and his rights," Tom stated.

"He's kingpin of the range tonight," said Latigo.

Two hours after dawn, voices brought Tom out of his uneasy sleep. Bowlings, the sheriff, stood beside the bed.

"Don't make me shoot you, Lucas," he growled.

Tom's gun belt was on a chair beside the bed. But two deputies were in the room with Bowlings. And Jim Watson, in bare feet, trousers, and an undershirt, stood helplessly in the doorway.

"They was in the house, Lucas, before I knowed what was up," Watson said unhappily.

"Forget it." Tom sat up. "This was bound to happen if I stayed around these parts. Bowlings, my leg isn't fit to ride."

"I brought a buggy," Bowlings said grimly. "And tell that side-winding sidekick of yours to take a tuck in his temper or I'll bring him along, too."

Another deputy brought Latigo into the room, ahead of a gun barrel.

Latigo was seething. "Tom, I oughta be dragged

through prickly pear for lettin' this happen. I knew I oughta stayed awake tonight."

"Go back to sleep," Tom advised calmly. "I might as well be taking it easy on a jail cot as in bed here."

Bowlings was irritable. "Don't come sneaking around the jail to get Lucas out," he warned Latigo.

"If I come, I'll send word so you can crawl in your hole," Latigo rapped out.

Bowlings drove the buggy. Five deputies sided them into town.

"You came heeled for me, I see," Tom commented. "Deputies, buggy and all. You must have been mighty sure I'd be at Jim Watson's."

"I had an idea," grunted Bowlings.

"Buggy looks like you knew I was wounded."

"I had an idea," said Bowlings again.

"How come?"

"I ain't talking," answered the sheriff.

Dry little Doc Schneider called at the jail to dress the leg. "It could be worse," was his tart decision. "Tore up your meat some, but it won't be worrying you when you get out of here."

Tom grinned. "My neck'll be worrying me then."

Doc Schneider was tired and his nerves were on edge. "This whole damned range has gone crazy," he burst out. "I been patching and cutting and sewing half of last night and all of today. The range is buzzing like a hornet's nest. Brett Canfield is the only sensible man I've seen. He says he's not taking sides and none of his men will mix in it."

Tom struck a match on the edge of the cot, lit the cigarette he had rolled, and bunched the pillow under his head.

"Brett Canfield never made a move that didn't gain something for Brett Canfield. He's a bunch of fancy clothes pulled over an icicle."

Doc Schneider closed his little black bag and grunted. "Might be better if everyone on the range was like him. I told Bob Hurley that, while I was dressing his leg, and got cussed out for my advice."

"Bob wounded?"

"In the thigh. He's laid out for some time. I told Miss Marcia to lock him in and sit tight if she had any sense."

"What'd she say?"

"Said she would," Doc Schneider answered brusquely as he left the cell. "But what chance has a mite of a girl like her to hobble that bunch of cut-throats and fire-eaters Bob Hurley has glued on his payroll?"

VII

Sometime before noon a loud banging on the cell door brought Tom awake, blinking and startled. A deputy had led Pete Salazar to the door. Pete's dark face was impassive. The droop of his eyelids was barely noticeable.

"No need for you to listen in," Tom said to the deputy.

"I guess it's all right, Lucas." But the deputy remained in the office doorway.

Pete's words were barely audible. "Thees Larsen . . . I follow las' night."

"Was he at Hurley's for the fight?"

"Oh, *sí*," said Pete. "That damned fight she's like to ron over me. But one, two hours later some Hurley men come home. They talk to thees Larsen by the corral. And he ride to Dry Forks, near the beeg cañon, and talk to one man there. Thees man I followed here to the sheriff."

Pete's Yaqui face was expressionless, but his black eyes were bright with excitement.

Tom, gripping the cell bars, snapped under his breath: "Who was the man?"

"*Señor* Canfield."

"Brett Canfield?"

Pete nodded.

Tom drew breath softly between his teeth. "Where's Canfield now?"

"He sleep in the hotel, and go toward Hurley's leetle while ago. *Dios*, jus' now I find where you are."

"Seen Latigo?"

"No, *señor*."

"Had any sleep?"

"No, *señor*."

"All right. Get some sleep around town. You did better than I hoped you would."

Tom forgot the throbbing in his leg as he lay flat on the jail cot and smoked cigarette after cigarette. Larsen's men must have told Larsen that Tom Lucas had been wounded at Watson's ranch. Then Larsen had taken the news to Brett Canfield. And Canfield had decided what to do. It looked as if Brett Canfield, the cool, dandified manager of the big XS Syndicate Ranch, who had said he was not taking sides, was in this up to his neck.

The red-headed deputy, Clancy, in charge of the jail today, brought in more news. Several of Hardesty's bunch had been killed and a dozen wounded. Hardesty hadn't been scratched. Fire-eaters like Hardesty were leading the hue and cry, were rounding up every man on the range who could carry a gun. The next time there would be no trap, no surprise. When they

65

were through, Bob Hurley's bitter, arrogant hide would be nailed for good.

Through the jail windows, Tom could sense growing excitement as riders from the range began to gather. Hurley men were staying inside their fences.

Tom thought of Marcia. She was there at the ranch, where the fighting would be. And she wouldn't leave, not with Old Bob Hurley wounded. Tom knew her too well to hope for that.

Latigo was allowed in, unarmed, watched by two deputies as he stood at the cell door.

Latigo was glum. "Tom, there ain't nothin' I can figure to do. Everybody allows you're caught cold. They say it'll have to be settled in court now. How's your leg?"

"Still on me," said Tom, sitting on the edge of the cot. "Seen Pete?"

"Yep."

"What do you think?"

"I'm studyin' what to do. Got any ideas?"

"Plenty . . . but they aren't any good. What I think and what I can prove are two different horses."

Latigo nodded morosely. "I'll look around. Might be I'll get an idea. I'm kinda glad you'll be in here tonight, Tom. The hell you've been preachin' against is sure gatherin' this time."

• • •

Before dark, gunfire broke out down the street. Men were whooping, shouting, hurrahing.

"Celebrating," Clancy answered Tom's query. "Brett Canfield is setting up the town."

Tom dropped his feet over the edge of the cot and sat up. "How come?"

Clancy gave him a peculiar look. "Canfield's marrying Bob Hurley's granddaughter tonight."

Tom said nothing. He could feel the blood pounding inside his head. He didn't know his teeth had bitten down hard on his lip.

Clancy went on awkwardly: "Looks like this'll stop the fighting. Canfield'll just about be running the Hurley Ranch from now on. Nobody's got any quarrel with him. Soon as he's married, the fight'll be called off."

Tom tried to swallow. His throat wouldn't work. And Clancy blundered on: "Preacher Gray is gonna marry 'em in church tonight, here in town. Canfield's promising a big dance and free liquor afterward. Some of the women folks has already gone out to ride in with the bride. Canfield asked 'em to, so he could stay here in town and get things ready."

"Damn you," said Tom hoarsely. "Get out of here!"

Daylight began to fade. Tom, still hunched on the edge of the cot, was shivering or trembling.

67

He felt numb. But his mind was racing. Marcia marrying Brett Canfield! Marcia in Canfield's arms! Marcia's lips against Canfield's lips!

Clancy brought in a tin plate of food and a cup of black coffee. A second deputy stood behind Clancy as the cell door was unlocked.

"Better eat something," Clancy advised gruffly.

Tom shook his head. "Bring me some soap and water," he said dully.

"Gettin' fixed up for the wedding?" The other deputy grinned.

"Shut up," snapped Clancy. "Get him some water and a towel and soap."

Tom washed, gave them back the soap and towel, and took the food. But he couldn't eat. He left the plate on the floor, rolled a cigarette, lay flat on the cot. Bowlings was not around the jail. Clancy had gone out. It was dark when the other deputy came for the food plate.

"Hell, you ain't et," he said, peering through the bars.

"I'm sick," Tom mumbled.

The deputy snickered. He was a lanky young relative of Bowlings, named Hawkins. He had his idea as to what was wrong with the prisoner.

"Your belly'll outweigh your heart if you hold off long enough," he said. "I'll leave the plate there. Won't be no more until morning."

"I'm sick," Tom muttered again.

"I reckon you won't die until Brett Canfield

gets married," Hawkins chortled as he left.

Canfield's wedding celebration was getting away to a noisy start. Marcia would have left home by now, riding the ranch road toward town, toward her wedding—toward Brett Canfield's arms. . . . Tom tossed on the cot, groaning. When he rolled off helplessly and lay twisting on the floor, the sound brought Hawkins investigating with a lamp.

The yellow lamplight picked out Tom writhing on the floor. Hawkins uttered an oath.

"What the hell's wrong with you?" Hawkins asked.

Tom's eyes were wide, staring. White froth bubbled on his lips.

"You got a fit?" Hawkins loudly demanded.

Tom doubled up, gasping, and the froth bubbled and sucked on his lips. His legs twitched and jerked.

Hawkins was alarmed. "Damn you!" he said angrily as he unlocked the cell door. "It'd be like you to kick off while I got charge of the jail. What'n hell's wrong with you, anyhow? You looked all right a while ago."

Hawkins entered the cell. He put the lamp on the floor and knelt by Tom.

With lightning speed, Tom's hand snatched the deputy's gun out of its holster, slammed it hard against the fellow's head. Half stunned, Hawkins fell back against the cot. Tom came off the floor

69

with a cat-like lunge that ignored the pain of his wounded leg and arm.

"I'll leave the grub for you," he grated. "I hope it tastes better than this soap I been chewing. If anybody asks you where I've gone, tell them I'm celebrating Brett Canfield's wedding."

Lucas used Hawkins's gun to club the deputy flat on the floor. Tom heaved the limp body onto the cot, face down. He buckled on Hawkins's gun belt, blew out the light, locked the cell door, limped into the jail office, and took a rifle out of the gun rack on the wall.

As he stepped outside, the first thing he saw was the horses that were tied in front of the jail. The street was dark. No one was watching the jail. Tom picked out a horse and rode out of town, unchallenged. He put the horse into a run as he passed the last houses.

Half an hour later he was on the Hurley Ranch road, riding hard. Pain tortured the wounded leg, and the bandage was soaked with blood, but Tom hardly knew it. This was the road Marcia would be riding toward her wedding. He had to see Marcia, who had lied to him with her lips, her eyes, and her words.

He might have missed her. She might have started early. She might be in town now, in church. She might even be making the responses in the ceremony that would make her the wife of Brett Canfield.

The moon was not up yet, and the road was dark when Tom galloped around the base of a small hill and met the wedding party. Half a dozen buggies and several riders were dimly visible in the starlight. They stopped as Tom galloped up.

"Who's that?" a man called, riding close to make out the stranger.

"Ain't you one of Canfield's men?" Tom asked.

"Yeah. Who is it?"

A second rider pressed close, with a biting exclamation: "Tom!"

That was Marcia, riding leather to her wedding. Marcia, dismayed, angry, scornful in her surprise.

Tom knocked the Canfield man groggy in the saddle. His horse swung short, crowding against Marcia's horse. Tom's good arm swept Marcia out of the saddle.

She fought him as they bolted off the road, leaving women's cries and the angry shouts of men behind. Shots were fired, wide of the mark, because of Marcia. Only one or two men attempted to follow them. Tom crowded Marcia across the saddle and fired back. He thought he heard a horse go down. He couldn't be sure.

They were bolting through piñon trees now. Branches were slapping at them out of the dark. And Marcia was fighting to free herself.

"I hate you for this, Tom Lucas! Oh, how I hate you!"

"You'd be hating Brett Canfield someday if he

stopped you from running off with the next man."

"Don't you say such things to me. You! With Bud's blood on your hands."

"That's all a lie. You know it."

"I believed you until Bud was killed. What a fool I was. You're everything low and despicable. Everything grandfather said you were. Brett will get you for this."

"Fancy clothes got your eye, didn't they?" shouted Tom. "You had to rush out and marry him before someone else got him."

"I love him. Do you hear me? I love him. Now put me down."

"Then you lied about loving me. You aren't the kind to change this quick. And I was fool enough to believe you. Tricking me. Putting blinders on me while you made a play for Brett Canfield."

"That isn't so. I told you the truth. I believed in you. I meant everything I said."

A piñon branch slashed Tom across the face like the sweep of a whip. He held Marcia and laughed as he raked the spurs.

"Then you still love me. You can't stop loving so quick. You know it's all a lie about Bud. Marcia, why did you do it? Why did you leave me when I needed you? Why did you bust the one thing I was living for? I wouldn't have hurt you like that. Day and night, I thought about you and dreamed about you. And when I was in a corner and needed you most, you turned to Brett

72

Canfield. I wouldn't have treated a strange dog like that, let alone someone I loved!"

Marcia had stopped struggling. Her arms caught him and clung. "Oh, Tom."

Marcia wept there against his chest. And Tom held her and asked huskily: "Why'd you do it, Marcia?"

"They told me there was no doubt you killed Bud. And Brett said today you were in jail, wounded from the fight last night. Tom, what could I think? If you had broken your promise not to fight us, everything else must be true. And Brett asked me again to marry him and said there would be a massacre tonight if something wasn't done. He showed me how I could stop it . . . by marrying him at once. Oh, Tom, it's cost us Bud. It has to stop. I thought you'd turned against me. All I had was Bud's grave . . . and the promise of more killing tonight."

"All you've got now," said Tom, "is me."

"I want to keep you," Marcia said unsteadily.

Tom stopped the horse and listened. The piñons loomed darkly about them. The horse was blowing hard; there were no more sounds. Tom felt blood in his boot, but it did not matter.

"Does your grandfather know you promised to marry Canfield?"

"No," said Marcia. "He's sick and helpless tonight. I told him to sleep. What will happen to him, Tom? What's going to happen to us?"

"You're running the ranch now, aren't you?"

"No," said Marcia wearily. "I thought I was, but I'm not. Before dark I paid off Larsen and the seven men he brought, and told them they could leave. They took the money . . . and then Larsen laughed at me and said they'd wait until there was a man to give them orders. When Billy Dangerfield tried to back me up, Larsen wounded him in the arm. He . . . he acts like he owns the ranch. Grandfather is too sick to hear about it. I'm helpless."

"No," said Tom. "Not helpless now. You've got a man."

"Tom, you can't go there."

"I'm already going," Tom said grimly.

VIII

They rode slowly across the sandy bends of Brandy Creek and crossed the Arroyo Hondo. By day, the sandstones there were yellow and red. Tonight the cold current from the foothills splashed about the horse's legs. They came through the piñon pines to the range west of the Hondo, where Old Bob Hurley had built his massive log and adobe buildings.

The windows of the big house were so cheerful with light it made it hard to believe Old Bob lay grievously wounded inside, or that the range

74

around was haunted with violence and with sudden death.

No one challenged them. The front door was open. Men were laughing and talking inside, instead of in the bunkhouse.

Bitterly Marcia whispered: "They're making themselves at home."

"Go in," said Tom under his breath. "Tell Larsen he's got to get out, *pronto*. And when I come in, you run straight to your grandfather's room and lock yourself in."

"Tom, I'm afraid. I can't have you hurt."

Tom kissed her.

"I'm already hurt," he said huskily. "And I'd be hurt worse if I didn't do this."

Marcia slipped to the ground and walked to the house without looking back. Tom swung down stiffly, flexed the fingers of his good hand to limber them, and drew the deputy's gun. He made sure that the loads were right. For a regretful moment he wished for Latigo. . . . But Latigo wasn't here.

Limping on a leg all fire and pain down to the blood-soaked boot, Tom walked to the portal. The windows of the long, low-ceilinged living room were open.

Larsen's angry voice was audible: "You don't mean to marry Canfield?"

"You heard me," Marcia said. "Now get your men out."

"You're a little fool. Canfield'll change your mind."

"Get out!"

Larsen laughed. "Go to your room. I'll send for Canfield. No . . . not in the old man's room. He's asleep. He don't want to see you."

There was a slight scuffle. Tom heard Marcia's low cry of pain. Limping on the stiff and bloody leg, he shouldered into the living room, his gun sweeping the hard-case crowd.

Larsen was near the other end of the room, twisting Marcia's arm as he forced her away from a door she was trying to reach. The other men in the room were grinning. There were nine of them, sitting, standing, making themselves at home.

"You don't know your mind tonight," Larsen said genially.

"Mister," rasped Tom, "I know *my* mind."

Larsen exploded into action before he saw who was speaking. His gun was out as he whirled. And Marcia was still there by him, close, almost too close to risk a shot.

Tom threw the shot from his big six-gun. He followed with another, so fast that Larsen's lurch from a shattered arm ended in a plunge to the floor. He was still falling when Tom's gun flicked over and blasted again, dropping a man near a front window who had snatched toward his holster.

"Reach 'em high!" Tom yelled. His fourth shot slammed at a bearded man across the room who was making a furtive reach for his gun. It was a belly shot, doubling up the bearded man, piling him on the floor, where he lay motionless.

"Two slugs left! Who gets them?"

Marcia had darted to the end of the room. She turned, bringing up a double-barreled shotgun, which had been leaning in the corner.

Her shaking voice cut through the haze of powder smoke: "I can get two with this, Tom."

Eyes rolled from Tom's smoking revolver to the shotgun. Hands went toward the ceiling. The men were still dazed by surprise, by the roaring shots, by the deadly accuracy of Tom's lightning-like marksmanship.

"Lady, watch that scatter-gun!" one of the men warned uneasily.

"Line up against the wall," Tom gritted.

A wounded man reached for the gun he had dropped as he fell. Tom kicked the gun away.

Then the bedroom door opened. Old Bob Hurley stepped into the room, clad in trousers and nightshirt. He came with a lurch of weakness and pain, two guns in his hands, his gray hair bristling above his bleak threatening face. Old and badly wounded, Bob Hurley stood wide-legged, fierce, exultant as he saw Tom.

"Lucas, I've finally got you. . . ."

Marcia cried: "Gramp, don't use that gun! Tom's helping us! I'm going to marry him!"

"Marry him? You're crazy, girl! You don't know what you're sayin'. I promised to get him for Bud. And I got him. What's the matter with these rabbits I hired to use their guns? What are they doin' here in the house, anyway?"

Tom answered him. "Don't ask why, you stubborn fool. Look at them. Did you think you could hire every cow thief, gunman, and outlaw in the territory and have them jump when you barked? These are Larsen's men. They're taking Larsen's orders. And Larsen, damn you, is taking Brett Canfield's orders. Use your head. You've started a range war. You've stirred up hell this range'll never forget. It's cost you Bud, killed Johnny Waite, made an outlaw out of me, and almost killed you. And all because you were too blind and stubborn to listen to reason. You had to be head bull of the range, tail up and pawing dirt when anyone looked cross-eyed at you. And what's it got you? Marcia almost married to Brett Canfield. Your ranch heading into the pockets of a bunch of owl-hoot raiders who've been leading you around with a nose pole. Now get back while I peel the guns off of these ranahans!"

Old Bob's shaggy brows drew down in a scowl as he looked at Marcia. "What's this about marrying Canfield?"

"Brett asked me the day I came back, Gramp." She was facing her grandfather, their eyes clashing.

"You told me that. And I told you to laugh at him," Old Bob said.

Tom tossed the gun belts he had collected into a chair near Marcia.

Marcia's voice shook. "Every man who can use a gun is gathering to cross our fences tonight. They're going to make sure no Hurley ever burns another rancher out. You started it. How are you going to finish it? Brett Canfield had an answer. They'd not ride against him and his wife. After you made me believe Tom had killed Bud, I told Brett I'd marry him . . . to stop it all. But Tom saved me from that. And he's here now to help you. Kill him? You should be on your knees thanking him. You've had your way and you've failed. . . . If you don't want us, we'll leave . . . and keep going."

IX

Tom had seen a proud old pine on the high slopes torn and bowed by the wind. He thought of that now as he watched Old Bob. Age seemed to have gathered heavily on Colonel Bob Hurley's shoulders.

Men from the bunkhouse were gathering out

front, tramping noisily into the hallway, crowding into the living room doorway.

"What's all the shooting about?" someone asked.

Old Bob faced them, and his shoulders went back. The harshness of authority rasped in his reply.

"Who asked you in here? When I want my hired hands in the house, I'll tell 'em to come. Get back to the bunkhouse or I'll gun whip the first man I get my hands on."

They gave back before that blast of anger, muttering and mumbling as they straggled out. And Old Bob dropped heavily into a chair. He gestured with one of the guns.

"Get them wounded men fixed up."

"First," Tom said, "I'll lock these owl-hoot jaybirds in the store cellar under the kitchen. Bring the shotgun, Marcia. Use it if you have to."

The store cellar under the kitchen was lined with rock, windowless, strong as a dungeon. The sullen prisoners filed down. When the last of them were in, Tom dropped the heavy plank door in the floor and locked it.

Marcia, standing in the kitchen doorway, spoke suddenly: "Tom, I hear a horse coming. It's galloping."

"I'll go out, honey. Turn down the lamps in the big room."

Tom blew out the hall lamp as he passed it.

The galloping horse stopped before the house as Tom stepped out on the portal.

Brett Canfield's voice sang out: "Larsen! Hey, Larsen!"

Through the open window, Larsen's labored warning came thickly: "Look out, Canfield! Lucas is comin' out to meet you!"

Tom was off the portal, in the starlight. Horse and rider were a dozen paces away. Brett Canfield opened fire instantly. Tom triggered one shot at that uncertain target, just as a fiery whip seemed to sear across his scalp, blotting out the night.

Dimly he sensed that he was falling face down, helplessly. He felt Canfield's foot stir him roughly, vaguely heard Canfield's voice: "Should have got it long ago, damn you."

Tom fought the numbness. His fingers clawed into the ground. Gradually he could move, stir. His hand struck the gun as he dropped. Holding it loosely, he got to a knee, staggered to his feet. His head was on fire from a raw, bleeding furrow. A quarter of an inch deeper, and his brains would have spattered out.

Canfield's angry voice came from the house: "What's the matter with you, Larsen?"

"Lucas gunned me."

"So you weren't man enough for him? Where's your men? Those fools from town are coming. They decided I was tricking them about the wedding. Hear that, Marcia? We've got to meet them and get them back to the wedding."

Tom reached the portal as Marcia cried: "I'd use this shotgun on you first! I know now that Larsen killed Bud. I know why. And now you've killed Tom. A gun would be too good for you!"

Canfield bawled his fury at Larsen: "I might have known you'd start talking if you got a bullet under your hide."

"You fool," was Larsen's weak, harsh answer. "I haven't said anything. But you've damned your own self now. Now you'll never get her or the ranch. A lot of good it did me to fix young Hurley and play your dirty game. If I swing for it, I'll see they knot another rope for your neck."

"Don't shoot him, Brett!" cried Marcia.

"He won't," came Old Bob's cold voice. "I can plug a dime from this chair with either gun. Stand still, Canfield, till I decide whether to kill you on account of Bud or let you hang."

Tom stood listening to a sound that had followed him into the house. Somewhere out in the night a low drumming thunder was rising. Horses, he decided. Many horses were galloping across the range toward them.

Warning shouts rose at the bunkhouse as Tom lurched through the living room doorway. One lamp was burning dimly in the big room. Larsen, on the floor, glared up at Canfield, who had lifted his hands. Old Bob was hunched in the chair, grim faced, thumbing back the hammers of his two guns. Marcia cried out and ran to Tom. She was still holding the shotgun.

"He didn't kill you. Oh, Tom, my dear," Marcia said with relief at sight of Tom.

Tom held her slender body close for an instant before he backed away.

"They're coming from town to clean out the place," he announced. "Get the lights out, windows closed, and the door locked. I'll do what I can outside."

"What can you do?" snorted Old Bob.

Hurley men ran into the house. There were six of them, all old hands, men who had been with Bob Hurley for years.

One of them snorted angrily: "Those new men figure they're licked. They're pullin' freight."

Tom had a sudden thought. Marcia had spoken of seven men coming on the payroll with Larsen. But nine men had been here in the house with Larsen.

"Hurley," Tom called, "who helped you put those half dollars under the calf hides?"

"Jake Knox and this dead skunk here on the floor!" growled Old Bob. "Thatcher's his name. He quit Canfield and came to work for me about a year ago. I've been sittin' here studyin' it. I reckon Canfield can tell how your brand got on those yearlings."

The thunder of hoofs was shaking the night.

"Close up the house!" Tom ordered. "Don't shoot unless you have to."

The last light went out as he limped dizzily outside. The night hid the approaching riders. A rifle barked out there—and then another. . . . A crackling wave of shots stormed from a long, ragged crescent of men riding toward the house.

Tom dropped flat near the portal. Lead whined overhead, slapped into the house walls, crashed through glass. Canfield's waiting horse bolted. A bullet sent it floundering down.

Tom shouted, but his voice was drowned by the crash of gunfire out there in the night. Even if his voice did reach a few of them, what good would it do? A hundred men formed an out-of-control mob, irresistible in its fury.

A great circle of riders surrounded the house now. The thunder of hoofs continued as the circle kept in motion, Indian fashion, gradually coming closer. They reached the haystacks, but no flames licked up. They were keeping the night dark.

Not even Marcia would have a chance if the house were fired. Blasts of lead were greeting every movement at windows or doors.

Tom's horse had been taken away. He'd be shot down if he tried to walk out to those shadowy riders.

An idea made him cup his hands to his mouth and shout: "Latigo! Latigo!"

A bullet sent dirt into his eyes. Ricocheting

lead ripped through the collar at the back of his neck, as he shouted again for Latigo. Tom knew that tall, gaunt man must be out there somewhere. Alone in town, seething against Bob Hurley, Latigo wouldn't hang back from this raid.

Again: "Latigo . . . Latigo!"

A bawling answer came out of the ring of moving riders: "Tom! That you, Tom?"

"Yes! Come closer!"

Latigo rode nearer. "What you doin' here, Tom?"

"Stop those fools, Latigo! I've got news for them!"

"I'll try, Tom."

Latigo rode back. His shout was audible. "Hold up, men! Lucas is there! Stop shootin'! Tom Lucas is comin' out!"

Slowly the gunfire began to slack off. Quiet crept back over the night, so that a man's voice could be heard.

Tom walked out from the house. Latigo rode to meet him and swung down from the saddle.

"My God, Tom, this is a hell of a place to find you. How come?"

Shadowy riders were closing in on them.

Tom shouted at them: "I rode here with Marcia Hurley, men. We're going to be married. Brett Canfield's in there with Bob Hurley's guns on him. Canfield's behind all this trouble. He had one of his men working here for over a year.

Larsen killed Bud Hurley. There won't be any trouble from the Hurley Ranch from now on. Climb down and talk it over!"

Cal Hardesty's angry voice yelled: "It's another trick, like Canfield's wedding. We came to clean out Hurley this time, and we aim to do it! Lucas, if you've throwed in with Hurley, take your medicine along with him!"

"Shut that fool up, Latigo," begged Tom.

"I'm kinda tired of him myself," said Latigo, swinging into the saddle.

Latigo rode through the gathering riders, toward Hardesty's loud voice.

"Never mind Lucas. Get on to the house, boys! We got . . . ," Hardesty's voice choked as it broke off in mid-sentence.

A man called: "Hey, what're you doin' to him?"

Latigo's answer was rich with satisfaction. "I've already done it. Let him stay there on the ground and cool off. All he's done is a lot of loud-mouthed talkin' to push us into trouble. Pay attention to Lucas, boys. He's talkin' sense tonight!"

The moon was rising. Objects were becoming plainer. Light steps came up behind Tom, and Marcia caught his arm as she faced the gathering mass of riders.

"Go back, Marcia."

"Here's where I belong, Tom."

Then—inside the house—two shots sounded.

"What're we waitin' for?" a man at the rear shouted angrily.

"They're shootin' at us, boys! Let 'em have it!"

"Wait!" Tom bawled.

Marcia began to tremble as she peered toward the house. Her fingers dug into Tom's arm.

"Tom! Grandfather's coming. They'll kill him out here."

Saddle leather creaked as men shifted warily to see what was happening. The waxing moonlight made the open space before the house like a ghostly stage—a stage on which Old Bob Hurley stalked out into the open alone.

Old Bob's gray hair was like a defiant crown. His hands still gripped the two, big single-action guns. Each step was an effort that every eye could witness. But his head was up, his shoulders were back, the old fierce pride was about him like a challenging shield.

"Here comes the old wolf! Now we got him!" shouted out from the mob.

Old Bob came on. The murmur and movement among the riders quieted. . . . Tom knew why. Men loved Old Bob or they hated and feared him. But always they respected him for that fierce pride of his, which never allowed compromise.

It was there now in every halting, painful moment. Like a scarred old wolf that knew no fear, Bob Hurley stalked out to face his enemies in the open.

He stopped, breathing hard, near Tom and Marcia. His voice was labored, but his words carried.

"You just heard Larsen shoot Brett Canfield. One of my men finished Larsen. Two thieves fell out, and they're both dead. Canfield wanted a ranch without working for it. Marrying the land was his way. He went after my Marcia as soon as she got back home. To get her, he had to make a skunk out of the man she liked best. You all know what happened to Tom Lucas. I was wrong. I played the fool. It's cost me my grandson. Canfield wanted all, so he had one of his hired gunmen kill Bud. . . . I'm getting old. Maybe I ain't been the kind of neighbor some of you like. Now I'm eatin' dirt. I'm asking for peace. . . . Not for me, but for my granddaughter."

"What's this about her gettin' married, Hurley?"

"She tells me she's going to marry Tom Lucas."

"Let 'em come into town and get married then, so we'll all know where we stand. We know Tom Lucas."

"No," said Bob Hurley, throwing up his head. "I'll give one more order and stand on it. When my Marcia brings me a new grandson, it'll be under my own roof. In the meantime, send for the preacher. Go get your women folks, and start the barbecue pits."

THE OUT TRAIL

Two days the blizzard had moaned over the barren lands. Two days Blanton and his dogs had slowly fought the weary miles, heading painfully and stubbornly into the whirling gusts of finely powdered snow crystals, sharp as blown beach sand. And in the afternoon of the second day disaster overtook them.

The dogs, plugging forward blindly, had struggled over the sharp crest of a spruce ridge. A balancing ledge of wind-blown snow had collapsed under them. Dogs, loaded sled, and Blanton at the gee pole, had crashed down the steep slope in the grip of a young avalanche. His body was forced one way, a snowshoe twisted the other. There was a sharp snap in his left ankle, a wave of excruciating pain. He came to a stop half buried in the snow, with the sickening realization that he had badly sprained the ankle, perhaps broken it.

Half a dozen yards away snarls, yelps, animated flurries of snow marked the dogs and sled. Blanton knocked the snow out of the fur-fringed hood of his parka, and yelled hoarsely at the dogs. Then he set himself painfully to wriggling out of his cold berth and bringing form out of chaos.

It took fifteen minutes of hard floundering work to dig out the heavily loaded sled and get the yelping dogs straightened in the tangle of harness. He was perspiring when he finished, and most of it was from pain. His ankle seemed on fire and was swelling rapidly.

He kicked off his snowshoes, slung them on his back, balanced on the sled runners and yelled at Mum, his big husky lead dog. Mum led off docilely enough, seeming ashamed of the bad judgment he had shown in striking that flimsy snow ledge. The snow had blown off the flat valley floor beyond the spruce ridge. The dogs made fast time across it.

In a balsam thicket several miles away, Blanton halted the dogs. The screen of thick conifer branches had stopped the snow; it was not deep behind them. While the dogs lay panting in their traces, Blanton got out his axe. Hobbling painfully, he found a dead tree trunk, cut out an armful of dry sticks, laced off some splinters.

A match from his waterproof packet put flame to the splinters; he soon had a crackling fire. Snow in a small tin bucket, a handful of tea in the water when it boiled, gave him tea. He gulped the raw, hot liquid, felt better for it, and proceeded to take stock of his injury.

The ankle was swollen badly. Each step brought blinding pain. He could do little traveling while it was in that condition. The bone did not seem broken, but it would take several days of perfect rest before it was safe to use it at all.

Several days—and the dog food would not last more than five longer. His own rations about that time. The Hudson's Bay post at Mulberry Portage was not less than two hundred and fifty miles away. Traveling light and fast, as he had been, he could just about have made it. Now, unable to break trail for the dogs, forced to add his hundred and eighty-five pounds of weight to the sled load, it would take many days longer. And every day he rested by the trail used up that much more food, lessened inexorably his chance of ever getting out.

The conifer branches whined and lashed uneasily as the blizzard plucked at them. One of the dogs howled dismally. Blanton drank the last of the tea, stowed the bucket, threw the crackling tip of his long, walrus-hide whip at the dogs, and pushed out into the teeth of the wind again.

Two hours later he was dizzy with the repeated shock of pain. It stabbed clear up to his hip each time he bore his weight on the ankle, or the sled gave a lurch. The wind still clawed at him, wailing out of the vast lonely stretches of the wilderness like disembodied souls fleeing from emptiness into emptiness. At times it seemed to laugh with malevolent glee, then mock stridently. Its cold breath disputed relentlessly each rod of the way.

The bald, savage loom of a black gneiss ridge thrust out abruptly into the valley floor. The trotting dogs swerved to the right, hunting for the end of it.

They were bearing to the left once more when Mum uttered a high-pitched dismal howl. The other dogs took it up. Something was ahead. Blanton strained his eyes but could see nothing. The uncanny senses of the malemutes were seldom wrong. Something was ahead. His heart leaped with hope. The cabin of some trapper or prospector perhaps, where there was shelter, warmth, food.

Beneath the mantling hood of his snow-caked parka his ears caught a faint answering chorus of yelps, drifting down on the wind. The dogs redoubled their cries, increased their pace.

There was someone ahead.

Five minutes later Blanton's straining eyes made out a bobbing string of dogs, a racing sled, a dark, hulking figure running effortlessly behind.

The load of worry went off his shoulders. The pain in his leg was forgotten for the moment as he eagerly watched the other outfit come up. The dogs were yelping eager challenges at the strange team, which was coming fast, bellies almost to the ground.

Like a ghost team in some strange dream it swept abreast. His own dogs slackened, turned expectantly. The running figure at the gee pole of the other sled lifted an arm. The long leather thong of a dog whip curled and cracked along the backs of the strange Huskies. Driven by that, they surged into the traces and whirled on by.

Stunned by the unexpectedness of it, Blanton shouted hoarsely: "Stop!"

He might as well have addressed one of the grotesque totem poles of the coast Indians. The hooded face of the stranger did not even turn in his direction. The arm raised again, throwing leather at the leaping dogs. Sled runners hissing softly on the snow, snowshoes scuffing in fast measured rhythm, the outfit passed on.

Blanton's dogs stopped, whining eagerly. He turned, sent another hoarse hail after the receding back of the stranger.

It had no effect.

And even as he looked, a veil of fine snow dropped down. The man, the sled, the dogs, grew dim, indistinct. Then vanished.

Blanton stood stupidly, wondering if he had dreamed it.

But the attitudes of his dogs belied that. An outfit had really passed him, running wildly ahead of the storm. An outfit that had broken all the tacit rules of the trail, the unwritten code of the Northland. It had failed to stop, ignored a call of distress.

Blanton's jaw clenched hard. He thought of his

rifle snugged under the canvas sled covering. A savage impulse to turn and follow the other swept through him.

Here in the great vacant lands of the north, life was stark, elemental, ruthless. Those who denied help when it was needed were apt to find themselves forced to give it. But his dogs were jaded, tired, no match for the animals of the stranger. They stood little chance of gaining on that mad pace.

For long moments Blanton waited there, hoping against hope that there had been some mistake, that the other would turn and appear once again. But only the mocking curtain of snow slanted past, and the wild wail of the storm chuckled at him.

Blanton went on, pondering the strange happening. Who was that great ghostly figure that had swept past so quickly? Why was he traveling so fast? Why hadn't he stopped?

Was he running from something? Had he killed, and was fleeing straight into the heart of the wilderness from the avenging hand of the law? If so, the law must be close behind to drive him so recklessly.

The light of the short winter day began to fail. Fever crept up his leg and into his body. And the pain was always there, harsh, cruel, relentless.

Blanton sang a little, laughed foolishly, wondered what the end would be. A creeping, wavering line of starving, exhausted dogs, falling in their traces finally? Long, helpless days of starvation, through perhaps another blizzard, culminating in the soft easy sleep of hunger and cold, from which there is no awakening? When the spring thaw came and the snow wasted away from the warming ground, would a grim heap of bones and clothing give a silent story to some passing Indian or trapper? It had often happened before. It might well be the fate awaiting him now.

He realized dully that he must make camp, erect a windbreak, eat and prepare for the night. He felt sick, nauseated. The dogs struck a patch of drifted snow. Their struggling forms seemed to waver grotesquely.

The eager howling of Mum snapped him back into clarity. Mum was swerving from the straight course he had been holding. Swerving to the left, toward some unseen definite object. It was off the trail, and yet Blanton let him go, caring little at the moment where they went. The nausea returned, grew stronger as they swept into a trail cut through the gaunt, silvery trunks of a belt of birch trees.

A quarter of a mile of that, and suddenly they were in the open again. Ahead lay a smooth, unbroken expanse that could be nothing but frozen, snow-covered lake surface. A whiff of smoke brought Blanton's head up, sniffing eagerly. The dogs swerved sharply along the lake shore, yelping loudly. Answering yelps came to meet them.

The low bulk of a log cabin thrust up suddenly, outbuildings scattered around it. A canoe shed, a storehouse, piles of winter wood. And the cabin with a drift of dark wood smoke writhing from the chimney, torn into shreds, and swallowed by the wind.

Two Huskies heaved out of the snow and stood baying defiance. Blanton's dogs rushed up and threw themselves on them. In an instant there was a tangle of dogs and harness, snarls, savage barks.

Blanton let them fight, too sick and weary to try and separate them. He staggered and hopped toward the door of the cabin. It remained closed despite the tumult outside it. Blanton's fur-mittened fingers found the catch. He wondered dully if the door was locked against him, the cabin empty in spite of the smoke.

And then the door flew open before his weight. He sprawled into a warm, dim room, scattering snow over the puncheon floor. And as he raised his head his jaw went slack and he stiffened.

Standing across the room were two figures—a man and a woman. The man held a rifle firmly in his hands, the muzzle covering Blanton steadily.

The greeting was so unexpected in this land of hospitality that Blanton did nothing but gape for a moment. And then he croaked: "Put that up. I need help."

The woman cried: "It's not LaBreese, Father!"

The gun muzzle lowered, the weapon was quickly set against the rounded logs of the wall. The man leaped across and caught his arms.

"Sorry," he apologized. "I was sure ye were someone else. What's the matter? Come over here. Sit down."

He helped Blanton to a chair made from willow branches, with a laced deerskin seat. Noticing Blanton hobble clumsily as he covered the several steps, he queried: "Something the matter with your foot?"

"Sprained or broke my ankle," Blanton panted. "Food low. Thought I wasn't going to make it to Mulberry Portage when my dogs spotted your cabin and brought me here. Guess you'll have to take care of my dogs. I can hardly stand."

The dogs were still fighting outside. The man sprang to the woodbox beside the stove, caught up a stick, threw a parka over his shoulders, and ran out, slamming the door against the biting cold. His shouting drifted in as he separated the dogs and unfastened them from the harness.

Blanton threw back the hood of his parka. His eyes were more accustomed to the light. He saw clearly for the first time the woman. She was young, slim, wearing a dark woolen skirt and a man's lumberjack. A mass of dark hair was piled high on her head. Her face was oval and regular, her skin darkened by the weather, but smooth. And there was rouge on her lips.

Rouge here in the wilderness! It had been many months since Blanton had seen the rouged lips of a woman. Any woman's lips for that matter, save those of Indian squaws. Somehow, they didn't count as women to his mind. They were part of the landscape.

He became conscious that he was staring rudely. She flushed slightly, turned her head away. He dropped his eyes, spoke matter-of-factly.

"I don't know how bad my ankle is. Feels like . . . like . . ."

"Like the very dickens?" she finished for him with a smile.

And then she did a thing he was not to forget for a long time. She went down on her knees before him and took hold of his damp, dirty shoe pack of caribou hide.

"We'll have a look at it and see how badly it is hurt," she said briskly.

Blanton helped her as best he could. They were peeling the heavy, woolen sock off the swollen ankle when the door opened, and the man came in. Blanton looked up and saw him clearly for the first time.

A man, he judged, in his early fifties. Hair already beginning to whiten. Frame short and rugged as the gneiss ridge he had passed back on the trail. There was a kindly look about the face. Little wrinkles radiated away from the corners of the eyes. There was little resemblance between the two of them. Father and daughter, from the way she had addressed him. She must take after her mother. Where was that mother? Blanton wondered.

The girl uttered a low cry of pity as she gazed at the swollen black-and-blue ankle.

"You did hurt it . . . badly!" she exclaimed. "You'll have to get to bed right away. I don't see how you got here with it in that condition."

"Rode the sled," Blanton explained. "It . . . it hurts a little." His lips grimaced with the pain of it.

She sprang up.

"I'll heat water. Father, help him into bed. He can use LaBreese's bunk."

There were skins on the floor, a caribou head over the stone fireplace, a small shelf of books along one wall, a table and chairs, two wall bunks, and a couple of doors opening off into other rooms.

One of them, he judged, was to her room, the other the kitchen. There was a rack of guns beside the fireplace, snowshoes and skis standing in one corner, and a pile of traps near the fireplace. The cabin of a trapper, Blanton decided as the older man helped him wriggle out of his parka and outer trousers and hop across to one of the bunks.

The older man stood considering him.

"My name," he said, "is Sanderson. James Sanderson. That is my daughter, Margaret."

"I'm Stanley Blanton, on my way out to Mulberry Portage," said Blanton.

The girl entered the room with a pan of steaming water. She set it on the floor and smiled sympathetically as Blanton put his foot in it gingerly and caught his breath at the hotness of it. When the foot was soaking in the water, Blanton told them bitterly of the racing figure that had passed him in the storm, ignoring his cry.

Father and daughter looked at each other. Blanton caught the impression of something between them, something under the surface that occupied their minds fully as much as his coming did.

Sanderson said slowly, after a moment's thought: "That would be LaBreese ye seen. The man I thought ye were when ye burst in the door."

"Who is he?"

"LaBreese was my partner."

"Oh."

Blanton asked nothing farther, seeing that here was a matter that was none of his business. Sanderson had said "was" in referring to his partner. Something had evidently happened to break the partnership.

Sanderson, evidently realizing that Blanton was curious, explained further, and there was in his tone regret and a trace of sorrow.

"It has been lonely here this winter. LaBreese has been acting queer. Getting sullen and suspicious. Today he harnessed the dogs and said he was going to yon side of the lake to look at one of the trap lines. I tried to get him to wait until the storm had stopped. He lost his head, cursed and raved. And then when I went out to get some wood, he took his rifle, stepped out the door, and shot at me. The bullet went through the flesh of my shoulder. . . ." Sanderson shrugged one shoulder.

Blanton remembered then that the older man had moved a trifle stiffly when helping him.

"It's lucky he didn't kill you," he commented.

Sanderson nodded.

"Perhaps if I had not dropped in the snow, behind a pile of wood, he would have. He thought I was dead. Margaret saw him take the gun and shoot. She slammed the door and barred it. LaBreese tried to get back in. When he could not do that, he left with the dogs and sled. We have not seen him since. It was not a sane man who passed you, Blanton. It was a madman, and only God knows what was in his mind or where he was going. You are lucky he did not shoot you."

Blanton recalled that looming hazy figure that

had raced past him on the wings of the storm, like a ghost. There had been something uncanny and unreal about it even then. Now, at the thought of the madman charging blindly through the vast empty wilderness, with the mocking moan of the storm finding a counterpart in the twisted fantasies of his brain, a cold feeling went down Blanton's spine.

What would the madman, LaBreese, do? Race ahead until his exhausted dogs fell in their traces, and stagger on until he met the same kind of death? Or would he range the barren lands with ready rifle and death for anyone who incurred the enmity of his distorted mind?

The thought, he saw now, weighed heavily on the minds of the two who stood by the bunk. LaBreese had suddenly become another factor in the ever-present threat of the wild.

Blanton smiled, said casually: "From the way he was traveling away from here, I doubt if he ever comes back to this part of the country again."

His assurance, he saw, made Margaret Sanderson feel slightly better. Yet when she presently brought bandages and carefully wrapped his swollen ankle, a frown of worry was etched again and again between her brows. And it was not on account of him or his ankle, Blanton knew. LaBreese was still on her mind.

He lay in the bunk and heard her presently

moving about the kitchen, preparing supper. The door was open. Now and then he caught glimpses of her sleeves rolled up over bare arms, face flushed from the heat, little tendrils of hair falling down about her cheeks.

He was strangely contented. The nearest outpost of civilization was hundreds of miles away; civilization as the outer world knew it hundreds of miles beyond that. And yet it seemed to him that in this small log cabin he had found civilization and comfort and happiness.

With Sanderson's help he managed to hobble to the table. They ate, the three of them. Caribou steaks and plump baked ptarmigan, fluffy biscuits, hot gravy, creamed peas—none the less delicious because they came out of a can—and dried-apple pie with a golden-brown crust.

Such food, after months of trail fare, seemed vastly better than any ever put out by the most expensive chefs of the Ritz. Blanton ate until he was gorged, and he laughed sheepishly as he pushed back his plate.

"Didn't mean to make such a pig of myself," he apologized. "I guess I lost control at the sight of such food."

Sanderson chuckled as he tamped tobacco in a stubby blackened pipe and applied a match to the bowl.

"A woman," he observed, "is a blessing."

Then, as if that remark had started a train of unpleasant thought, he frowned as he sucked on the pipe. "This country isn't the best place for them," he added. "One canna tell what's goin' to happen."

Blanton slept restlessly that night, turning and muttering in his sleep, at times waking up with the pain in his ankle. Once he opened his eyes with a start and became aware of a small figure, tallow candle in hand, two big braids of hair down the back of a blue dressing gown, standing by the bunk surveying him.

"Does it hurt?" her voice asked sympathetically. A small hand touched his hot forehead.

Blanton smiled drowsily.

"I'm all right," he muttered. "Go back to sleep."

And strangely he did feel better. After the door to her room had closed behind her, he drifted into sound sleep that lasted the rest of the night. A psychologist might have found something significant in that; Blanton didn't.

He was aware, as he lay in the bunk after breakfast next morning, of contentment. The trail over the hill seemed far away. He wanted nothing more than he had now.

Sanderson brought wood to the woodbox beside the small sheet-iron stove, letting in a shaft of crystal sunlight, clear and flawless as a fragment of rare mineral. The blizzard had passed in the night and Nature seemed eager to make amends for the fury of the preceding days.

Sanderson stopped beside the bunk, tapping tobacco in his blackish pipe with a blunt forefinger, considering Blanton gravely.

"LaBreese took his dog team and sled," he said abruptly. "He shot all my dogs but two, and they aren't much good."

"My team is outside," Blanton offered.

Sanderson nodded seriously.

"I was thinkin' o' them. Our trap lines are too much for one man. I consider it a brave pity for good animals to waste in the traps."

"Use my dogs for anything you care to."

Sanderson continued to regard him gravely. "There is the matter o' leavin' you alone with Margaret," he said slowly.

"Of course, if you feel that way about it . . . ," Blanton flushed.

Sanderson raised a protesting hand. "It is LaBreese I'm thinkin' of."

"I'll be here."

"True," Sanderson agreed after a moment's reflection. "In three days, wi' good weather, I can be back from the east swing. I will do it." He raised his voice. "Margaret girl, come here."

She heard her father's decision calmly, and just as calmly helped him get ready, and stood in the doorway and waved to him as his figure shuffled off down the lake after Blanton's sled and dogs.

Her face was grave as she came in and barred the door. Blanton knew by that act that LaBreese was still on her mind also.

She wore different clothes today. White woolens, soft, fleecy, with a dash of style that surprised him.

"You didn't shop at a trading post," he commented.

She smiled, as a mother might at the naïve remark of a child.

"I put them on for you," she told him. The matter-of-factness of the remark robbed it of any coquetry. "There aren't many young men to wear clothes for in this country," she added.

He chuckled, rubbed ruefully at the stubble on his cheeks, and asked for a mirror. His lips puckered in a whistle of dismay when he saw his reflection.

"More hot water," he begged. "And my razor kit there in the corner."

She brought them. He shaved, combed his hair, even managed the one wrinkled necktie he had intended wearing back.

"Now," he said triumphantly when she came back into the room.

She inspected him critically, and then said honestly: "I wouldn't have believed it. You look ten years younger and . . . and . . ."

"And?"

"And almost handsome."

"Almost?" he mocked.

They laughed.

During the day they talked in snatches as she moved about the cabin, cleaning, cooking, and in the afternoon sewing. He learned that she had been in the north country two years. Her father had been there twelve, except for brief trips out to see his family in Montreal. Eight of those twelve years he and LaBreese had trapped together, doing well. The mother had died. Sanderson had brought the daughter into the north woods, that she not be alone and unprotected.

"And how do you like it?" Blanton asked curiously.

She was sewing at the moment. Her eyes went to the window through which could be seen a glimpse of the birches lining the lake shore to the south, and a patch of azure sky.

"I like the woods," she said slowly. "And . . . Father wants me here." A breath, that was almost a sigh, slipped from her. "Sometimes when I think of the world outside . . . the cities, the people, the things they are doing . . . it seems like the current of a mighty river rushing some place for some purpose. Here it is a backwater, with hardly an eddy." Her glance went to him and she smiled apologetically. "Sometimes," she confessed, "I want to go with the current and take my chances of drowning."

Blanton nodded. "I know the feeling. I think that's what brought me out ahead of time. I'd been in the backwater too long."

He told her of himself and his partner, two mining engineers, who had been carried by plane into the far hinterland where white men rarely penetrated. For a year and a half, they had charted the mineral resources of the region for a great mining syndicate.

The supply plane had failed to come. His partner had died from pneumonia. The atmosphere of desolation that had closed down about the isolated camp, and the lack of supplies, coupled with an unprecedented absence of game, had crystallized his decision to strike for the outposts of civilization.

Margaret Sanderson told him quickly: "About six weeks ago an airplane flew over, going north. It didn't stop. We didn't see it come back. It was a big, red plane."

Blanton exclaimed: "That must have been the supply plane that didn't come! I wonder if it crashed. Poor devils! And Joe and I were cursing them for forgetting us."

"Death seems to go with this country, doesn't it?"

"No more than anywhere else," he defended.

"I suppose it seems harsher because we have to face it alone."

"Probably. We're through with death, I hope."

They talked in a lighter vein the rest of that day, and the next.

On the morning of the third day his ankle was better. He tried it, found he could limp about. He insisted on bringing in wood.

At the woodpile Blanton stood in the bright sunlight, looking about. The utter stillness of the Northland lay heavy. Sunshine glistened on the smooth expanse of the lake. Roundabout the birches stood dark against the snow. *Like an enclosing wall,* Blanton thought.

His mind went back to the wistful look in the eyes of Margaret Sanderson when she spoke of the "outside". She was lonely. He knew the feeling. It was not a matter of company, of people about, such as her father and the man LaBreese.

He was conscious of a lingering regret that in a few days he would be heading out, and she would be here by the lonely lake, with the birches ringing densely around.

His mind was still on that as he piled wood high in the crook of his arm and turned toward the cabin. He heard Sanderson's two old Huskies burst into vicious barking. The soft crunch of snowshoes warned him. He looked over the top of the wood—at the hulking form of a stranger before the cabin doorway.

LaBreese, the madman, had returned!

He was a huge man, bigger than Blanton, muffled in trail clothes and greasy parka. A ragged beard matted his face. A pair of wild-looking eyes glared along the rifle he had raised to his shoulder.

In that moment Blanton knew the feeling of death, close and certain.

"Put that down!" he yelled, halting.

LaBreese wavered an instant, and then leaped into the cabin. Guns and supplies were in there, and Margaret Sanderson. Shaking a little from the narrow escape, Blanton limped swiftly to the door and entered.

Margaret was standing near the stove, eyes wide, face pale. LaBreese had his back to the gun rack, where he could watch her and the door. He was gnawing nervously at his bearded lip. His face, in the sheltering hood of the parka, which he had not yet thrown back, looked dark and foreboding.

Blanton, with a wary eye on the rifle in the madman's hands, limped to the woodbox and dropped the wood in it.

"You're LaBreese, aren't you?" he asked casually, turning.

"Who tell you?" LaBreese demanded suspiciously.

"Sanderson told me you had gone out on a short trip and he was expecting you back any hour."

LaBreese laughed. "You t'ink to trick me, eh?" he rumbled. "I know you are police come for me. Sanderson called you."

"I'm only a prospector," Blanton told him. "Ask Sanderson when he returns."

LaBreese laughed again. And in that laugh were things beyond the pale of human emotions. He fumbled inside his parka, brought out a long, keen hunting knife. Point first, he flicked it to the floor. It stuck upright, quivering. The handle was of horn, curiously carved.

"That's Father's knife!" Margaret cried. "He carried it away with him! Where did you get that, LaBreese?"

"I kill him and his dogs," LaBreese stated with vast satisfaction. "He is out on my sled. Now I kill you and dis police . . . and burn down everyt'ing. And den LaBreese go 'way where dey never find him." With a wide sweep of his arm LaBreese indicated the far, back country.

Margaret looked at that knife, still quivering slightly, and suddenly her slim frame shook with a dry sob.

Blanton felt cold and icy, watching her and LeBreese, the madman. Sanderson was dead, he did not doubt, waylaid as he mushed on the homeward trail. And what was to prevent LaBreese from carrying out the plan born in the dark recesses of his distorted brain? He estimated the distance between them. LaBreese could easily shoot him down before he closed in. And he had no weapon.

He had been vaguely conscious of a low, far-

113

away hum, like a swarm of bees, or the wind in the balsam tops. It grew more distinct. Blanton wheeled toward the doorway abruptly.

"That's an airplane!" he exclaimed. "Perhaps it's coming here."

LaBreese made a warning gesture with the rifle.

"Don' go out!" he ordered.

They waited, listening to the growing hum become the roar of evenly firing cylinders overhead. There came no break in the steady rhythm, no indication of the plane descending. It passed on into the north and disappeared. With it went hope.

"Must be another plane trying to get in to Joe and myself," Blanton muttered.

"Sit down!" LaBreese snapped at him. And when Blanton had slowly obeyed, LaBreese said to Margaret: "I am weary and hongry. You will cook for me, and you will bot' help me pack. Den I will kill you and set fire to dis and go 'way. Cook me much food now."

With a despairing glance at Blanton, Margaret walked into the kitchen. He could hear her freshening the fire, moving about her ordered tasks deliberately. And he knew that her mind was groping blindly through its grief for some way to circumvent LaBreese's mad plan.

Each time he moved, LaBreese's eyes went to him watchfully. When the meal was ready, LaBreese ordered them to the south wall of the room with their faces toward it. He laid the rifle on the table and noisily wolfed the meal.

"*Sacre!*" he exclaimed when he had finished. "I 'ave change my mind, *mademoiselle*. I will take you to cook my meals. Now we will pack. Come, bot' of you."

Hot anger seared Blanton as he saw the pallor on her face grow deeper. Death one could face, but not living bondage as the chattel of a madman. And as he silently set about following LaBreese's orders, he knew that would not come to pass while he lived. She had given him kindness and casualness; something more than that was stirring in him. A psychologist could have told him about that, too. Blanton knew it only as hate of LaBreese, and dogged determination to seize his chance when it came.

But as the day wore on, it seemed there would be no moments when LaBreese could not easily drop him with a bullet at an instant's notice. LaBreese herded the two of them cunningly, from room to room, out to the stanch storehouse where sugar, flour, salt, tea, bacon, frozen fish for the dogs, and other supplies were kept safe from the marauding visits of thievish carcajous, hungry wolves, and other furtive denizens of the woods.

There were bundles of furs in there, too. Fine prime pelts worth top prices outside. LaBreese paid no attention to them. His mind had reverted to the elementals of life. Now and then he muttered in his beard, and his rifle jerked in his grasp, as if he intended using it any moment.

Such moments Blanton's scalp tightened and he made ready to spend recklessly his last moments. Each time, however, LaBreese held off, and the work of packing for a long trip went on. LaBreese had left his sled and dogs back in the trees. He made Margaret and Blanton don snowshoes, drove them to that spot, while he brought the sled to the cabin, with its still burden lashed carelessly under a fold of canvas.

Margaret Sanderson looked once, and kept her eyes averted after that. Silent tears started from her eyes and trickled unheeded down her cheeks. To Blanton fell the task of unloading the sled and laying the burden tenderly aside in the snow. He drew the canvas over it, a terrible anger growing in him as he saw her sway slightly and then stand waiting.

Then followed the packing of the big sled, LaBreese's blanket roll and hers, food and supplies, the thousand and one things that were to stand between them and the wilds.

All that took time. LaBreese seemed in no hurry. When the final lashing was in place, the brief northern day was partly gone. LaBreese herded them inside, and ordered another meal cooked.

He rumbled in his matted beard as he finally finished. "It is well. I can go in peace."

He stepped to the sheet-iron stove and kicked it over. Burning brands spilled out over the floor. A cloud of blue wood smoke surged up and mushroomed under the low ceiling. The dry floor caught quickly. LaBreese hastened it by kicking the table and chairs on the conflagration.

The crackling flames were affecting him with growing excitement.

"Burn everyt'ing!" he shouted. With a sweep of his arm he indicated the contents of the room.

Sanderson's knife still lay on the floor. There had been no chance to get near it, so close had been the cunning scrutiny of those mad eyes. Blanton's gaze went to it now. LaBreese was near it, watching him. In despair he tried to think of a way to distract the big man's attention for a moment.

His eye went to his pack, in the corner. His heart began to pound as an idea was born. He walked to the pack and caught it up.

"Burn everything," he agreed, tossing the pack into the center of the flames. "It'll make a big fire while it lasts, LaBreese."

"And you will burn wit' it," LaBreese said, coughing as a swirl of smoke struck him in the face.

The canvas pack covering flared up. The contents began to burn. Blanton watched it feverishly.

The heat grew intense. Smoke filled the room. Margaret had retreated toward the doorway. LaBreese ignored her. His eyes were on Blanton. The rifle was jerking in his fingers. He was gnawing his lip again. The mad flare of insanity grew in his eyes.

"You come for me, and for dat I kill you!" he shouted.

He lifted his rifle. In that moment a shot sounded behind him. Then another and another. LaBreese whirled.

Blanton, waiting for that, dove for the knife on the floor. His fingers closed around the carved horn handle as a fusillade of shots filled the room. Bullets whistled and thudded into the log walls. Blanton's pack spewed sparks as a box of cartridges inside ignited from the heat.

LaBreese saw what it was and whirled back as Blanton came up with the knife. Blanton's outstretched arm slapped against the rifle as LaBreese fired. He felt the bullet fan his cheek. He slashed with the knife.

LaBreese uttered a howl as one hand was rendered helpless. With the other he swung the rifle barrel. Blanton parried it awkwardly and closed in to slash again. LaBreese leaped back through the smoke like a big cat.

It was a strange and terrible scene, the two of them parrying, dodging while the smoke swirled thick about them, the hungry flames leaped high, staccato explosions drummed from the blazing pack.

LaBreese parried a knife blow with the rifle barrel and cast the weapon in Blanton's face. He caught Blanton's wrist and hurled his weight in. Blanton's weak ankle gave. Helplessly he lurched sidewise.

And as despair rushed over Blanton, LaBreese staggered and went limp. It was LaBreese who slumped helplessly to the floor. From a small hole in the side of his head blood began to flow. A bullet zipped past Blanton's face. Another from the same source that had struck down LaBreese.

Seizing LaBreese by an arm, he dragged him outside. Margaret was waiting there.

Her voice shook as she cried: "Look!" She pointed up.

A big red plane was winging down in a tight spiral over the smooth lake. As they looked, it landed evenly on its skis and taxied to shore.

Two men leaped out and ran to the burning cabin. Cochet, the pilot, an old friend of Blanton's, recognized him and pumped his hand.

"What the devil are you doing here?" he cried. "We found your camp deserted. Where's your partner? We tried to get in about six weeks ago and bad weather turned us back. When we found an empty camp today, we didn't know what to think. And what's the matter here?"

Blanton quickly explained what had started him

119

outside, and what lay behind the burning cabin at their backs. The flames had eaten through the roof and were leaping high.

"Lucky we saw the smoke and came down for a look-see," Cochet declared. "We can take you out now. You'll want to go, too, won't you, Miss Sanderson? The plane's light. We can take your furs."

Margaret hesitated, and looked at Blanton with dismay.

"I'm almost afraid to go," she confessed. "I have no one out there now. It's terrifying to think of the bigness of it, when you are alone."

"But you won't be alone," Blanton said gently.

Cochet laughed. "That sounds like a proposal."

"It is," said Blanton. "And will you two grinning hyenas go to the devil?"

"We'll do better than that," said Cochet. "We'll graciously turn our backs."

He had his reward a few moments later. Margaret said to him in a small voice: "Thank you. I . . . I'm ready to go now."

POWDER FOR
SANTA ANNA

I

That small thin old man must have known my answer before we sat in the dim back room of Papa Pio's café in Havana. He must have known my bitterness. Seven years of memories smoldered no less in this July of 1846 than in the first year.

"I'm not your man," I said, and I added, "sir."

He might have been a Boston trader planning Yankee traps for the fat Chinese merchants of the Canton Hong syndicate. He was Commodore Dexter, U.S. Navy. His blue eyes were hard as boarding steel. I was Cass Morgan, in business from the Guinea Coast of Africa to the Caribbean and the Mexican Gulf.

"Why should I risk my neck as a civilian in this war with Mexico?" I asked him. "I own the *Blue Turk* and the brig *Sampson*. I work with Irish O'Malley of New Orleans and the Isle of Pines. He gave me my start after the Navy threw me out. I'm doing well. And the men you want me to cross would throw me to the sharks."

The commodore tasted his brandy with the delicacy of a connoisseur and nodded. "They're rascals," he said, eyeing me stonily. "Scum, slave traders, gun-runners. Aye, and pirates, too, no doubt."

"The court-martial put me on my own," I reminded him. "Let the Army and your Navy have their fight in this war. I'll take care of Cass Morgan."

"*Our* Navy," he said. Then: "You were a midshipman on the *Constitution*. I was junior lieutenant on her, under Hull, in Eighteen Twelve." He looked at me. "You heard her beat to quarters, as I heard her beat when Hull cleared for action with the *Guerriere*. Now we're at war again."

"I'm sorry," I said.

"My granddaughter, Treva, thought you'd refuse to help the Navy," the commodore said quietly.

I was indifferent. "Treva's married, I suppose? To that Army fellow I had the trouble with . . . Lieutenant David Key."

"Treva's twenty-three now," the commodore said. "Old enough to know her own mind. Perhaps she and David will do something about it this fall. They're both in New Orleans. David is on duty, and Treva is visiting her aunt, Madame Oliveras."

I was silent.

"You put a sword scar on young Key's face that he'll carry to the grave," the commodore went on. "Got yourself court-martialed. Came close to involving Treva in talk. Damned foolishness in headstrong young roosters. You might have made first lieutenant in this war, if you'd kept your head seven years ago."

His thin old face was seamed and weathered. Men high in Navy and government trusted him. To me he was the tall masts and the ranked gun batteries, blood and bone of the fleet.

But I was young and hard with seven years of reckless living. "It doesn't matter," I said. "I'm doing well."

"General Taylor has won at Palo Alto and Resaca de la Palma," he said. "Taylor is at Matamoras, at the mouth of the Rio Grande, calling for supplies and men. Navy must move them. Navy must also stop blockade-running of war supplies to Mexico. We must know who tries to run the blockade, and where to catch them. Some will probably be Americans."

"Perhaps," I said, "men like O'Malley or myself?"

"Perhaps." The commodore stood up and laid a thin oiled-silk packet on the table between us. "If you should change your mind, and be boarded by one of our ships, while working for us, you might need this paper. You'll have no standing, of course, under the Laws of War."

"I'm a rascal, and I stay a rascal, even if I help the Navy." I smiled bitterly. "How do you know I won't use these papers while I'm running the blockade myself, with arms for Mexico?"

"I don't," he said. "Good day, sir."

• • •

The *volantes* were thick on the Paseo Tacon that night. High in front, the Havana carriages carried Negro postilions in big boots and gaudy uniforms, and ladies in white, with roses at their ears and languorous fans in their graceful hands. A man could be overwhelmed by that passing stream of beauty.

I hardly looked as my own *volante* rolled to Granville Crosby's house. I was thinking of Treva Dexter. I wondered if Treva's eyes could still flash as scornfully at anyone who had disgraced Navy epaulettes and Articles. I wondered if she was still as lovely.

In Granville Crosby's large square courtyard, I wondered why I had been invited tonight. Crosby was a tall Englishman, smooth as Jamaica treacle. The better Britons ignored him. His business affairs were vague and profitable.

Thirty-odd guests were in the drawing room, dancing, talking, drinking wine served by scarlet-clad Negroes. Crosby gave me a warm hand-shake.

"You'll have champagne?" he suggested, and he beckoned to a servant.

An hour later I was wishing Commodore Dexter were with me. As choice rascals as ever wore fine broadcloth and frilled linen were in the group about me. At my right was Macintosh, a pious Scotsman whose friendship was pure

126

poison, as I'd known trusting fools to discover. Spreck, the thick-necked Dutchman, had shot a man for truthfully calling him a Guinea Coast slaver. Varillat, the white-haired Creole banker from New Orleans, stood with all the wiry ease of a fencing master in Exchange Alley. The two Mexican gentlemen I did not know. Nor did I know Scofield, the beefy merchant from New York. Ramón Rodriguez was an elegant and shady Havana politician and lawyer, with a sly twinkle at life. I had always rather liked Rodriguez.

It was the champagne and the music, I suppose. "Gentlemen," I said, lifting my glass, "to the Lion of Mexico, to Santa Anna, the exiled president, who, I hear, is being returned to Veracruz, through the American blockade, to more honors and fame in Mexico."

Spreck's heavy chuckle assented. "To dot I drink."

"And," I finished the toast, "to all the men who will die in this unhappy war."

Spreck's wine suddenly seemed to gag him. The others looked glum. I laughed at them, knowing more about them. "To glory, then." I changed the toast. "And to profit."

I left them, smiling wryly as I went onto an outside balcony. I stared into the moonlight on the harbor, suddenly tired of Havana's narrow streets and lush nights. I thought again of Treva

Dexter and of David Key, together in New Orleans. Treva hadn't forgotten me, and all that she remembered of me was bad.

The girl who joined me on the balcony seemed startled at finding me there.

"From the back, *Don* Cass, you looked like *Señor* Crosby."

Susanne Valverde, singer and dancer in many countries, was considered beautiful by most men. She was, I suppose, with the humor that seemed to linger around her generous mouth and glow in the olive delicacy of her features. But I like better the fire of living, which always seemed so much a part of her. She had a dancer's graceful slenderness, soft blue-black hair, small and expressive hands. A French mother and a Spanish father had given her a zest for life like fine champagne, dry, tangy, with restless bubbles.

"Did you really think I was Crosby?" I asked.

"No," said Susanne. "But you might have pretended I did. Why don't you like me, Cass Morgan?"

Her nearness was heady. In the moonlight she looked young, innocent, desirable, in her high-waisted gown of cream-colored silk.

"I do like you, so I'm cautious."

Susanne turned her head. She was smiling a little. "We're so much alike, Cass. Always your kind and my kind must have what we want. Even if we're afraid of it. Even if we know better."

128

"Do you want Crosby as much as he seems to want you?" I tried to change the subject.

"Does it matter?" Susanne shivered slightly, and she looked at me again. "That Spreck is a bad man to do business with, Cass."

"I have no business with Spreck."

"And you will not have?" She put her hand on my arm, and the heady nearness of her was over me again.

"What are you trying to tell me, Susanne?"

Behind us in the balcony doorway, Granville Crosby's amused voice said: "Tell me also, Susanne. It should be interesting."

Susanne's fingers tightened on my arm, but she was laughing as she turned. "I'm trying to tell Mister Morgan that I want to waltz. He'd rather talk."

"In that case," said Crosby lightly, "let me offer myself. Morgan, I think one of the guests wishes to talk to you. Jan Spreck."

"Later?" I said to Susanne.

"Perhaps," she said airily. "But you must always listen to me, *Señor* Morgan. Closely. Or I promise you regrets."

So she warned me again as she left, and I wondered why.

Jan Spreck joined me a moment later. He was patting a handkerchief on his broad face and his thick neck, inside the points of his high collar. He was a massive man, with blond hair curling thickly over large ears. He always seemed to be perspiring and smelling of gin.

"For one year I will pay high for all the shipping space dot you and your partner, Irish O'Malley, have," he said. "Cash in advance. My own captains and crews. In three years, Mister Morgan, you will nod make so profitable a trade."

I laughed at him. "When your captains and crews come aboard our boats, we'll have small-shot and cutlasses waiting for them."

The big man sighed. He looked reproachful, hurt. "You haf heard lies, young man. All lies. I represent a contract with your government. . . . You do not believe? Wait here."

He returned with Scofield, the red-faced New York merchant. Scofield gave me the same assurance. Mississippi river boats were bringing vast quantities of supplies to New Orleans and would bring increasing quantities. Shipping was badly needed for cargo to General Taylor, on the Río Grande.

"Sir," said Scofield earnestly, "it will be a patriotic service. The profit, of course, will be handsome."

Jan Spreck beamed like an honest Amsterdam burgher. I thought of Macintosh, and Varillat, the slippery Creole banker, and of Granville Crosby. Something was wrong. Susanne had been trying to tell me of this.

"Irish O'Malley and I have other plans," I said.

Scofield was vastly disappointed. Spreck reddened and held his tongue. He was a cold-blooded and ruthless man, and never more so than when brooding like this behind his phlegmatic stare.

One of the scarlet-clad Negroes came to the balcony doorway and addressed me in Spanish. "*Señor*, a gentleman wishes to see you in the courtyard."

I took my leave, and went out wondering who would be seeking me tonight.

It was Sam Caffrey, captain of my brig *Sampson*, due from Barbados. Irish O'Malley had told me I was a fool to hire him. "I don't like the look in his eye," O'Malley had said.

Tonight Sam Caffrey, who usually dressed the dandy, wore a shabby pea jacket, too small, and patched trousers that a foremast hand would have scorned.

"I've lost the brig," he said in a nervous, hang-dog manner. He swallowed. "On a reef near the Cayo Cantiles. We were being chased by a Spanish sloop of war, and were on the reef before 'twas seen."

My graceful, fast-sailing brig, bought with profits of risk and careful planning! And I had intended to sail for New Orleans on her!

"What were you doing in there near the Isle of Pines?" I demanded coldly. "You should have been standing out to clear the Pines and Cape

San Antonio, before you made for Havana."

"A bit of private business," Caffrey said, still with the hang-dog look. "A little private venture of my own."

"Slaves," I said. "Don't lie to me, Caffrey. You took slaves aboard, against my orders."

"Only eleven," he admitted miserably. "Got 'em dirt cheap from a schooner that'd lost a mast and couldn't sail."

"I was warned against you!" I said, and knocked him down.

Caffrey got to his feet without spirit, one arm raised defensively. "Wait," he begged hoarsely. "The Spaniard got the slaves and some of the crew. They were searching the Isle of Pines for the rest of us. I got across the island and escaped in a fishing boat. If they catch me now, I'll go to La Cabana dungeons for slaving. I've known men who stayed in that hell pit for years, Mister Morgan. I've got to get out of Havana." A look of cunning came into his eyes. "If they make me swear the venture belonged to you, they'll have you for slaving," he added.

I wanted to knock him down again, but I held myself in check. The rascal might make trouble. Spanish law took strange twists.

"Go to my lodgings at Pio's place," I told him, "and wait for me. Put on some of my clothes, or the watch will pick you up, the way you look. Here's money for a carriage, and for Pio's silence."

I went back up to the broad gallery overlooking the courtyard. Jan Spreck was standing there, big, immobile, blank-faced.

"Dot mind of yours iss not changed, young man?"

"No," I said shortly, and went inside, wondering if Spreck had heard any of my words with Caffrey. Spreck would not be above sending a man to La Cabana dungeons for the same things he had done himself.

I waited for a dance with Susanne Valverde, and as we swung into a waltz, she asked: "You have not done business tonight?"

"Why shouldn't I?"

"A woman's whim." She laughed.

I was never quite sure when she was mocking me. The perfume of her nearness, her hair, the warm firm clasp of her fingers, her red lips and her slender grace, pushed sober thinking aside, made me breathe faster and draw her closer.

"Susanne."

"Yes, Cass?"

"You *are* beautiful."

"You've never said so before."

"I've thought so. Someday I'll tell you all the things I've thought."

"Someday?" Susanne said, looking up at me.

I don't know what she saw in my look. Her eyes dropped. I would not have thought Susanne could blush so delicately, or that she could draw away so naturally, like an innocent girl caught by confusion. Then I remembered she was an actress who had danced in the great cities of the world. She was no stranger to compliments. O'Malley had warned me about her. "Look out, my boy," he'd said. "Susanne has broken better hearts than yours." This was folly and I wanted none of it.

So I said: "I'm leaving for New Orleans in the morning." And the moment passed from us, and we were merely Crosby's guests, waltzing on his marble floor.

"I'm glad you're going, Cass," Susanne told me, and she would not say more when I tried to draw her out. Her last words were: "I think Irish O'Malley needs you, Cass."

I laughed at the idea of O'Malley ever needing anyone. O'Malley was fifteen years my senior, and never unsure of himself.

Many kinds of men stopped at Papa Pio's place. This night, when a *volante* brought me from Crosby's house, the driver looked ahead in the night, and exclaimed: "*Señor*, there is trouble!"

Men stood ahead of us in the warm, thick shadows, and as I left the *volante*, Papa Pio's waddling figure met me.

"*Señor* Morgan, how could I know of this? What could I do?"

"What happened, Pio?"

Pio elbowed ahead of me through the small

crowd and threw one fat arm out dramatically. A ragged Negro was holding a smoky lantern over a huddled body. The dead man was Sam Caffrey, wearing my clothes, and he had been stabbed in the back.

It was late that night before I slept. Murder was not uncommon in these dark streets near Havana's waterfront. But why had Sam Caffrey been killed so soon after talking to me? I was not satisfied that robbery was the reason.

In the morning Pio entered my room, panting from the steep stairs. His heavy mustache was jerking with excitement.

"This stranger," he said breathlessly, "asked for one small rum, and when he paid, he said it was bad that the *Señor* Morgan was killed last night."

I forgot the shirt I was drawing on. "A stranger down there thinks *I* was stabbed last night?"

"*Sí sí.*"

"What sort of man is he?"

"A Havanan, *señor*. A small man I have not seen before. Not an honest man, I tell you. He was surprised to hear that you were alive."

"Damnation! You told him I was alive? You're a fool, Pio. Is the fellow down there now?"

"No. He left quickly." Pio made the sign of the cross. "*Señor*, I am not the fool. Last night the man wearing your clothes was mistaken for you." Pio drew a fat forefinger across his throat. "No?"

"Breakfast, Pio," I said.

When Pio went out, I stood with the shirt half on, thinking of Jan Spreck on that shadowy upper gallery while I talked with Sam Caffrey. The threads of a web seemed to be closing about me. I wondered how much Susanne Valverde knew about it.

II

That afternoon the three-masted paddle steamer *India Star* moved slowly out past Morro Castle. I was on her deck as the pale blue and red Havana houses dropped astern, and the white bastions and rose-colored walls of La Cabana fortress followed.

My fellow passengers were Cubans, Spaniards, a Dutchman from Curacao, Englishmen, Americans, and Louisiana planters and Creoles from New Orleans, and among all the polyglot company I could find no one who showed interest in me.

Dead calm held from the Morro battery to the mud flats at the mouth of the Mississippi. The weather was hot, sultry. In the Mississippi current it became worse.

Early one afternoon two full-rigged ships came down the river in tow of steam tugs. They were Army transports carrying troops to General

Taylor. I watched gloomily. I was against this war with Mexico. Dispatches out of the north had painted a picture of mounting excitement in the States. Regiments of one-year volunteers were hurriedly being raised. The Caribbean countries were seething with excitement. Good men were dying, because politicians chose not to agree.

The oppressive heat grew worse under a greasy sky. Heavy scents of wild blossoms drifted from the riverbanks. Alligators slid smoothly off mud banks. Night fell solidly and blackly, and livid lightning began to flicker in the distance.

The storm approached. Wind began to sing through the high rigging. Officers shouted orders. Passengers had retreated below, but I was still on deck as the first hard sheets of rain drove through the black night.

I stood at the rail, facing the storm, and its very fury gave me an elation I needed. Lightning flashed blue-white and brilliant, and I turned instinctively from the bolt. That movement saved my head from the full crushing blow that struck at me from behind and drove me reeling against the rail. Only by instinct did I duck away from a second blow. My head came hard into a man's chest, and we staggered against the rail.

Lightning glared again. I sighted another man close on my left, his knife ready. I wrenched away to meet the threat of that knife, and I was clubbed again, and hurled over the rail. The next instant I went deep into the river and the deep-threshing paddle wheel overwhelmed me. One blade struck me, and the blow, tremendous and paralyzing, drove me down toward oblivion.

Some vague will to survive kept me from trying to breathe there under the water, made me struggle in the wild currents, and when it seemed I would have to breathe or die, I was hurled to the surface.

In dazzling lightning, the high stern of the *India Star* moved away like a vast black wall. A clap of thunder beat back my cry. I was strangling, half dead. But even then, I was furious at having dropped my guard in the last few hours. Sam Caffrey's death, while wearing my clothes, had been warning enough of danger ahead.

Susanne Valverde had tried to warn me, and I knew now that the mystery I had shrugged off was as deadly as death itself. What it was, I didn't know. But I would live to find out. I made that promise deep inside. I'd live and discover the meaning of all this.

A long time later I floundered weakly through soft mud and shallows and fell exhausted among wet reeds and grass. The storm had moved on. My head, my side, and right leg hurt, but I was alive. The knife had slit through my shirt and gashed across the ribs. Fever chills shook me for the first time in months.

But slowly I drew strength from the fact that

I was alive. I thought of Irish O'Malley in New Orleans, all unsuspecting of what was happening. The men who had tried to kill me were on the *India Star*. By morning they would be in New Orleans with O'Malley. We were partners. If death reached for me, it was also reaching for O'Malley. He must be warned.

Frogs chorused in the storm-washed night. Clouds of mosquitoes shrilled above me. Harsh birds echoed across the river. Then I heard dogs barking, and I struggled up and hobbled over the levee bank.

In returning moonlight, cane fields and woodland stretched away. The dogs were on a narrow road at the foot of the levee. A creaking ox cart was following them. The fever had me light-headed as I hobbled to the road just as the ponderous yoked beasts brought the great cart slowly to the spot.

"I must get to New Orleans," I told the Negro in the cart. "I'll pay to be carried there. I've had an accident."

The moonlight gleamed on his white teeth. "We goin' N'Awleans, suh. Slow-like, but we gets dere. Sack o' straw behin' de seat, jes' right fo' sleepin'. I he'p you on, suh."

It was a strange journey through a giddy, pain-filled night. At times I must have been out of my head with the fever. Once I caught myself

139

singing. But before dawn I slept soundly.

The bright sun woke me up. We were in New Orleans, creaking into the clutter, the hustle and bustle of the French Market. Here all New Orleans came to shop, look, gossip.

The world was swimming when the Negro helped me down from the high cart. I gave him money and lurched off through the market crowd in search of a carriage.

Fish, fruits of all kinds, were piled about. The loud bargaining, the people, the talk and gestures, were unreal as I went by. I had the feeling I was alone in the sick haze, and that I must keep going to O'Malley. I had to find Irish O'Malley and warn him that death might be waiting at any turn of the narrow streets.

Faces, faces without end, swam before my eyes—and then one face took form like a vision striking through the fever. All the world held only one girl like her, one girl with chestnut hair above the cool, clear triangle of her face.

"Treva!" I exclaimed. "Treva Dexter!" And then, as she looked at me with startled recognition, I laughed. "It's been a long time, Treva. Seven years."

A white-haired Negro with a basket moved watchfully to Treva's side. People were looking at us. Treva's voice trembled. "Cass, you're in trouble or drunk." Her voice became husky. "You've been bleeding!"

I looked down at my muddy trousers and my slashed and blood-stiffened shirt.

"A drunken, bleeding desperado is what you expected, isn't it?" I asked, and I laughed again. This was a dream, a nightmare, with strange faces watching curiously.

A little old woman, erect and purposeful in a black dress, joined Treva. Her brisk question had the faint music of French and Creole accent. "What is this, Treva?"

"Madame Oliveras?" I guessed. "Treva's aunt? Allow me, *madame*. Cass Morgan, once and always the devoted admirer of your niece." I bowed to her, and then fell flat on my face there in the French Market.

The next thing I saw was sunshine on the coverlet of a large canopied bed, where I lay. Madame Oliveras was standing at the foot of the bed, looking at me.

"So! Now we will live," she said. Her smile had the shrewd understanding of age. "Eleven days, *m'sieur*, we have tried to keep you alive. I think only a very wicked young man could have cheated the devil as you have. Treva was horrified at the things you said while in the fevers."

Alarmed, I asked: "What did I say?"

Her eyes danced. "How delightfully wicked you have been, *M'sieur* Cass Morgan. Like

141

M'sieur Lafitte, that handsome pirate who lived on Bourbon Street when I was younger."

"*Madame*, I am *not* a pirate."

"*Oui, m'sieur.*"

Then I thought of O'Malley. Eleven days had been lost. O'Malley had not been warned. He might be dead.

"You have been too kind, *madame*. I must leave at once. There is a man I must see."

"If the man is in New Orleans, we will send for him," she said firmly. "You have not recovered. *M'sieur le docteur* will say when you may leave."

"My friend is named Irish O'Malley. Word can be had of him at the Bank of New France." And then I asked: "Is Treva here?"

"Treva, *m'sieur*, has gone to the plantation."

She must have seen my face fall, because she added: "She waited until you were out of danger." And she went out, smiling faintly to herself.

Within the hour I heard O'Malley's gusty laugh in the rooms below, and his deep voice cried: "Strangle me, ma'am, but I thought he was dead! Best news I've had for years."

Then he was in the doorway, towering behind Madame Oliveras. Tough as mast cable, with a sun-blackened face, a square jaw, and a wide mouth, O'Malley was so near to being ugly that he was almost handsome. He came in like a gust of fresh life, a fine Panama hat crushed under one arm, and his other big hand reaching for my hand.

Madame Oliveras retired. O'Malley grinned down at me. "I talked with men who'd seen you on the *India Star*."

"I had a bit of trouble downriver. Went overboard."

"Gambling, or a woman?"

"I'm not sure what's back of it. I made shore with my head cracked and the fever loose again. Didn't know much until today."

O'Malley looked about the room. "Nice nest, but I need you. Our boats are on the government run to Mexico."

"By any chance, have you met a man named Scofield?" I asked.

O'Malley's laugh boomed out in the quiet room. "Scofield's pockets hold the easiest money we'll make in many a year." He spun a satin-covered chair to the bed and sat down, explaining.

Scofield had arrived in New Orleans four days ago and gone at once to O'Malley. The general commanding at New Orleans Barracks had vouched for Scofield. And now our boats were in the war, subject to official orders.

"Jan Spreck was with Scofield in Havana," I said. "Spreck spoke to me for Scofield, and I turned them down."

"So Scofield said," O'Malley admitted, grinning broadly. "I thought better of the matter than you did, Cass. Now get out of that fancy bed and pull rope."

But Irish O'Malley was holding something back. After he left, I had the tight and troubled feeling that we were both deep in that web I'd suspected at Granville Crosby's house in Havana. But now it was worse. O'Malley was not fully at my side. That, I think, troubled me more than anything else.

III

O'Malley had rooms for us on Bourbon Street, and two days later I moved in with him. Over a bottle of fine old Portuguese port, O'Malley said: "General Santa Anna has left Havana on the British steamer *Arab*, sailing to Veracruz. It's a fool thing to let happen. Santa Anna will rally Mexico. Taylor will need more supplies. We'll have work ahead." He stood up, chuckling. "I'll leave you now, Cass. I'm calling on your pretty friend, Susanne Valverde."

"The devil! Is she here?"

"Her dancing makes the soldiers and officers bug-eyed every night at the theater." He winked broadly. "I haven't told Susanne you've been living off the fat of the land, with an old flame to soothe your fever."

"Blast your insinuations. Tell Susanne I expect to see her."

O'Malley had first introduced me to Susanne.

His humor now had warning. "Our pretty Susanne will make you dance before she's through, and you won't like the tune, my hearty. Mind your step."

I laughed.

That night I sat in the theater and watched Susanne dance. She was a lithe, slender girl, in a full, flaring skirt with a yellow and white *tignon* on her head. Behind her an old black crone hunkered beside an iron pot and fondled a snake. Three black men knelt in reeds beside the crone, and their low chant and the soft rhythm of the small drums they thumped went on and on.

Susanne glided across the stage and saw the snake. She retreated in alarm and posed uncertainly. The drums began to thump faster, faster. . . . Then she began to dance, and as the drums and the chanting came louder and faster, the packed theater filled with savage under-currents straight out of the African jungle. I had heard it like this in the slave barracoons on the Guinea Coast. It was old Africa, the wild and passionate outpouring of the deepest voodoo jungle. Only Susanne Valverde, I think, could have made it seem so real. When the curtain was lowered, proud Creoles and gold-braided officers clapped madly.

Later, in a swaying barouche which carried us to a famous restaurant, Susanne sat beside me, slender and smiling.

"You have the jungle behind that pretty face," I said.

She was pleased. "You like it, Cass?"

"I'm not afraid of it," I said, and she laughed.

Jacques had my order beforehand. The champagne was iced and ready. Candles lighted our table in an intimate corner. And when we were seated, I said: "Did you know that the captain of my brig was stabbed to death that last night in Havana? He was mistaken for me. And I was followed from Havana, and almost killed as the boat came upriver?"

Susanne's hand was unsteady as she put the fragile wine glass down. "No, Cass."

"Why did it happen?" I demanded, leaning forward.

"I don't know, Cass."

I laughed at her. It was the wrong thing to have done. Her quick, flashing anger was like the barbaric fire in her dance.

"Don't laugh at me, Cass Morgan! I warned you in Havana. And here you are in New Orleans doing business with Jan Spreck."

"With the government, and that man Scofield. What do you know about Spreck's business, Susanne?"

"Go ask the voodoo women back of Congo Square!" she threw at me. "If you won't listen to me, find a black witch you'll believe!"

Her cheeks were flushed and her eyes were

bright. She was beautiful as she raged in the candlelight, and I saw I would get nothing from her.

"Irish O'Malley made the deal with Scofield," I said sulkily.

"I know," she said. "Now please be nice."

When a carriage brought us to the house on the Rue Royale, where Susanne was staying, we were laughing light-heartedly as I handed her out on the banquette.

She unlocked the massive patio door. We stepped inside, and the heavy door swung shut, and we were alone and close in the dark shadows. A fountain tinkled softly. Perfume from flowers and Susanne's nearness crept about us. It was very quiet, and I felt the slow, hard thumping of my heart, the warmth of wine and Susanne running through me.

Her low voice said: "You'll try to keep from danger, Cass?"

"Why should you care, Susanne?"

The delicate oval of her face was close, looking up at me. "I don't want you to be hurt, Cass."

"Why not?" My heart was thumping faster.

"I like you, Cass." It was almost a whisper. "I shouldn't, should I? I don't know why I do."

I reached for her hand. Her small fingers were stiff, and then soft and submissive, clinging.

"You're more beautiful than ever," I said unsteadily.

She tried to draw away. Once more her reaction was like convent innocence, alarmed, confused, as though she didn't understand herself. I held her and captured her other hand.

"This evening has been so nice, Cass. I will see you again, won't I?" she said unsteadily.

"I'm here now," I said. "Look up, Susanne."

I brought her to me as she looked up. She was tense in the imprisonment of my arms. One small hand went to my chest in protest. She looked away as I bent to her face. I kissed her ear and the fragrance of her hair was giddy. The curve of her cheek was soft as I kissed her again.

Her whisper was barely audible. "Please, Cass. Please! We're too much alike."

I brought her close, hard. She began to tremble; she looked up and I found her mouth and there was madness in the soft, feverish hunger that met my lips. Her arms went around me. Her slender body was suddenly all sweet and yielding in the fierce embrace in which I caught her.

"Cass! Oh, Cass!" she gasped, as we clung tighter, tighter.

She had warned me we were too much alike. There was no city, no patio, no night, in those long furious moments that we clung together. No thought, no reason. Only the wild and elemental feeling that ran like fire and fever through us. Only the feel of Susanne's mouth, the hot touch of her cheek against my burning cheek, the utter yielding of her lithe and slender body against my hunger.

Too much alike, too wild and reckless to mean the things we felt. Suddenly I could almost hear Irish O'Malley's voice jeering: *"You won't like the tune, my hearty. Mind your step."*

I released Susanne.

"I'm ashamed, Cass!" she gasped. "Terribly ashamed."

O'Malley's warning faded. No woman, however gifted, could pretend such passion. None, however worldly, could fake such sweet confusion.

I brought her close again, gently, and kissed her tenderly.

But she disengaged herself, stepped forward, and pushed open the patio door. "Good night, Cass."

She closed the door quietly, and as I walked through the soft dark night I remembered Treva Dexter standing in the French Market in startled uncertainty. I could almost hear Treva's shaking voice saying: *You're in trouble or drunk, Cass.*

"Both, evidently," I muttered aloud. "And a fool besides."

I did not find the two men who had tried to kill me on the *India Star*. On an afternoon when I knocked on the door of the dignified Oliveras house, on Toulouse Street, the tall black servant

149

faced me politely and informed me that Madame Oliveras and the young mistress had gone visiting to Natchez.

I thought, as I walked away, that Treva Dexter might be escaping from New Orleans, where it was possible that we might meet again. How much, I wondered, was she running from the past between us?

In September, British sources brought word that General Santa Anna had made triumphant entry into the City of Mexico. The politicians in Washington had guessed wrong. They had let Santa Anna return, hoping he would rend Mexico into factions, after his exile. He was bringing the country together in fiery purpose. The war with Mexico promised to grow stubborn and long.

O'Malley and I had become forwarders of freight—boxes, crates, dismantled supply wagons, harness, and all the assorted supplies of a fighting army. We obeyed orders, brushed elbows with the Navy and were prodded by the Army. New Orleans grew more busy and prosperous. Uniforms were everywhere.

Madame Oliveras and Treva were still visiting upriver. Between Susanne and myself lay a truce. We were, I think, on guard against each other.

One afternoon, while O'Malley and I walked to Government Wharf, through the levee smells of molasses, tarred cordage, hides, and spices, O'Malley said: "There's a Captain David Key been put working close with us. Ain't he the one you marked on the cheek?"

"Yes. So he's a captain now?"

"And not liking you any better, I'm thinking," said O'Malley. "Watch him. He's naming cargo that we carry."

"I'll not bother to think of him," I said, and I went with O'Malley aboard O'Malley's two-masted schooner, *Voodoo Belle*, just in from the Río Grande.

Mongo Jack Walker, the bearded captain of the *Voodoo Belle*, had been a slaver. He was a man after O'Malley's heart, with big scarred fists used on many a wild crew. In the small cabin, Mongo Jack opened a bottle.

"Drink and be damned, gents, as the preacher promised. What'll I take next to old Taylor?"

"Powder," I told him. "You were due ten days ago, Captain Walker. What delayed you?"

O'Malley chuckled. "No doubt a bad norther, Mongo, eh?"

"Bad weather she was," Mongo agreed, showing strong white teeth. "East to s'east wind in our faces all the way home, gents."

I left them a few minutes later and walked forward, where some of the hands were working under the squinting gaze of Holly, the mate.

A gray-haired seaman was coiling rope near Holly. I went over to him. "Nice trip?" I asked.

"Middlin', sir," he mumbled.

"Bad weather, I hear."

Mongo Jack spoke harshly behind me: "Show one of the owners politeness, damn you! Tell Mister Morgan about that dirty norther that caught us, and the head winds we bucked."

"Never mind," I said. "Thank you, Captain, for your interest."

"Always thinkin' of me owners, sir," Mongo said, grinning.

O'Malley was in the background. "Friend of yours coming aboard, Cass," he warned.

It was David Key. Seven years had only stamped deeper on David's aristocratic face all the frigid self-assurance of his distinguished New England background. The last time I had seen that face, blood from my sword cut had been streaming past the thin mouth. The white scar from temple to jaw began to turn red now as we met face to face on the *Voodoo Belle*'s deck.

"Mister Morgan," David said coldly.

"So it's Captain Key now?" I said.

He nodded. "I've had the feeling, Mister Morgan, we'd meet again. I've heard of you from time to time." His voice held a faint, icy contempt. "A colorful life you've been leading."

Somehow, I'd thought the bitterness had stayed only with me. David had remained an officer and a gentleman. His welcome had remained with Treva Dexter, over whom we had fought. He had kept everything, and I had lost everything. But he was bitter, too. Seven years later, here in New Orleans, he hated me.

"At least," I said, "I've had my share of fighting, David. Not checking supply lists and fighting a war with blobs of ink."

David froze. He had to swallow twice before he said in a stifled voice: "I've applied for a place in the battle regiments. A quartermaster's assignment was not my seeking, sir. I'll be out of it, if possible. Meanwhile, I'll do my duty. . . . Gentlemen, this schooner was expected some time ago. General Taylor is advancing on Monterrey and needs his powder."

"Captain Walker will explain his slow voyage, no doubt," I said. "You'll excuse me."

Key ignored me.

I walked to the French Market for coffee and a chance to think. There I saw Madame Oliveras and Treva again.

I bought roses from a flower seller and took them to Treva. She was boy-slim in a high-waisted dress and wearing a gay bonnet.

"Why, Cass!" she exclaimed, and she took the roses before she thought, and color came into her face.

"So, *M'sieur* Pirate!" Madame Oliveras greeted me.

"With your permission, *madame*," I said,

bowing, "I will call to thank you for your hospitality."

"*M'sieur*, in three days from now you must dine with us. Is it not so, Treva?"

"Whatever you say, Aunt Cecilia," said Treva coolly.

After that, in spite of Treva's coolness, I would not have believed trouble possible. Powder was being rushed into the *Voodoo Belle*. O'Malley was busy, and I was not much good to him. Treva was on my mind most of the time. I was thinking of her as walked on Chartres Street the third afternoon, and met Seymour Ashford, merchant and plantation owner.

"Here's luck," Ashford greeted me. Then he drew me under an overhanging balcony and looked around before he spoke. "Would you be knowin' of slaves that might be comin' in cheap?"

"No," I said shortly. "We're busy with supplies to Taylor's army."

He smirked. "Word comes up the bayous that boats still slip in at Passe de Terre and Isle Grosse. Smoke still makes signals on that coast."

"Damn the smoke signals, Ashford! I told you O'Malley and I were running cargo to the Río Grande."

He wagged his head, grinning slyly. "I've heard of a man who might be doubtin' that. He's talked with my overseer at Crooked Bayou. A Yankee stranger with a fine scar across his cheek, and he's traveled almost to Passe de Terre."

"The coast is full of Yankee strangers," I said, and I was sure Ashford looked disappointed as we parted. He had thought I'd be concerned, and I was.

A shabby *fiacre* hurried me to the levee, where the Navy sloop *Vandoria* was just back from the Mexican watch. I went aboard.

"I'll speak to the lieutenant," I told the marine guard, nodding at the officer near the mainmast.

The lieutenant turned. It was Jock Peters, once a midshipman with me.

"What a sight for blotty eyes!" he cried, rushing to shake my hand.

In seven years I had not stood on a man-o'-war's deck. I looked at the rubbed and polished guns inside their ports, the well-stoned deck, the rope ends, Navy-style, in Flemish coils. The glazed brim of Jock's cap, the rotten-stone brilliance of his buttons, the bright gold of his epaulettes, brought a tightening to my throat.

"I've only time to look at your pea-ball batteries and ask how the weather's been toward the Río Grande," I said.

"We'll lob broadsides with any three-decker," Jock swore, his round face shining. "As for the weather, I've never had a finer run. We're carrying dispatches to Mexico these days."

"No northers?"

"Nary one."

Mongo Tack Walker had lied about his weather, and O'Malley had all but suggested the lie to Mongo. David Key had known what he was about in the swamps to the south. Smoke signals must still be rising from Isle Grosse and boats putting in by Passe de Terre. I sent regrets to Madame Oliveras for not being able to dine.

The sun was still shining that afternoon when I rode south from New Orleans into the swamp country.

Big Jules, the overseer at Seymour Ashford's Crooked Bayou plantation, lived alone, loutish and brutal. Slaves and trade goods were smuggled through the swamps from the coast, and taken from Crooked Bayou to Ashford, in New Orleans.

That night, in the crude plantation house, Big Jules leaned his arms on a table and grinned through lantern light.

"The same two niggers who fetched you in last year will take you to the coast," he said, and winked. "Cargo comin'?"

"There'll be no cargo back," I said.

Jimbo and Sam were my swamp guides. A *pirogue* hollowed from a cypress log carried us into the swamps where channels were choked with masses of lush water hyacinths, and runaway slaves and half-wild men of the coastal wilderness lurked and hid.

Near sunset we camped on higher ground beside a cypress swamp, and we ate dried shrimp gumbo and corn cakes from the fire ashes. While the black boys slept like weary animals, I smoked a Cuban cigar by the smudge fire.

A bull alligator bellowed not far away, and then a low and drawling voice spoke behind me. "Sit easy, mister."

I knew the casual way a knife or a bullet could kill. I sat motionless while a blanket dropped over my head. "Damn these skeeters," the soft voice said. "Keg Head, you got him fanged. Bulltick, git them other two in the boat."

They lashed my wrists behind and helped me into what seemed my own *pirogue*. After what seemed like hours we were hailed. The boat touched land. I was guided ashore and the blanket stripped off. Smudge fires glowed. My soft-voiced man was an army sergeant, with sandy stubble. And the next thing I saw was David Key, immaculate, even here in the swamp night.

"A smuggler and a slaver," Key said contemptuously. "A man who'd help the enemy in time of war for dirty gold to spend on some cheap dancer!"

"You're a filthy liar, Key," I said.

"You'll hang," Key said. "After I investigate

Isle Grosse, you'll hang, Cass Morgan. Sergeant, I hold you responsible for him."

That night I slept little. At dawn we went on in three large rowboats of shallow draught, with small masts unshipped and lashed out of the way.

All that long day we traveled south, and the next day also, and late afternoon we followed a narrow channel into a long salt-water lagoon. Masts were stepped; we sailed on into a mile-wide bay and landed on a long point of land that thrust out from the west. The spot was some twelve miles east of Passe de Terre and Isle Grosse.

Here by the Gulf I sensed again the full depth of Key's cold determination. There had been about time for the *Voodoo Belle* to clear the Mississippi Passes with her powder cargo, and to put in at Isle Grosse. When he had proved she was smuggling, he meant to see me hang.

I still had hidden on my person the oiled-silk packet that Commodore Dexter had given me. I could have shown the paper to Key. I could have sworn anything we found at Isle Grosse was part of my plan to help the Navy. But the commodore had put me on my honor. He still believed in my honor.

We marched at dark along the ocean beach, west. Passe de Terre was a mile-long, sickle-shaped bank of sand that connected Isle Grosse to the mainland. At low tide the Passe lay under water that could be waded.

The channel into Grosse Bay was at the west point of Isle Grosse. Inside that western point of the island, a schooner could be tied almost against the steep shore. Palmetto brush and trees made a screen against boats passing offshore.

When we came over the beach sand to the Passe de Terre, Key's order was curt: "Muskets ready. We may be sighted before we reach the island. Any man who falters or turns back will be shot."

IV

My arms were lashed behind, as were the arms of the two Negroes, Sam and Jimbo. The sergeant kept watchfully at our heels. We waded out across Passe de Terre, and the dark mass of Isle Grosse grew clearer.

Sam's head cocked. I wondered what his swamp-trained ears had heard. And then from the undergrowth at the island's edge, came a shout.

"What do ye want?"

Key called the order. A shot rang out from the bushes; a few Army muskets answered. But that was all. The yelling soldiers made the island sand and crashed into the undergrowth.

I could have told them that two guards had usually been posted at this end of the island. One had run to give warning when we first appeared on the Passe; the other had fired on us.

"To the other end of the island!" Key cried.

"Mister," my sergeant warned me, "I'm watchin' you!"

Branches slapped at my face as the skirmish line advanced. In the scrub growth, moonlight was cut off. There was no warning that reinforcements had reached the lone guard until several guns suddenly fired at us.

The Army muskets replied. A soldier cried out in pain, and the troops plunged ahead. The guns of the island men retreated.

I stumbled heavily to the ground. "Git up!" the sergeant ordered fiercely. "Git up or I'll shoot!"

I leaped up and drove my head into his face. His musket seared flame past my shoulder, but I knew he'd have bayonet steel in my back as I ran.

I barely saw the black shadow that dove past me. It struck, head first, in the sergeant's middle. He doubled with a stifled groan and went to the ground.

"Kill 'im, sah?" Sam panted, rolling up on short, ungainly legs.

"Leave him. This way," I ordered.

The two Negroes and I plunged into the brush. Minutes later we burst out on the beach. "Get a shell and cut these ropes," I told them.

Sam backed to me with a wave-washed shell in

160

his strong fingers, and the sharp edge chewed at my wrist ropes and freed me. I used the shell on Sam and let him free the other black.

The night shivered with a deep report as I led them at a run along the beach. The *Voodoo Belle* was firing ball or cannister into the island undergrowth from a deck cannon. An American boat, firing on American soldiers, in time of war! O'Malley's boat, and so, in a way, my boat. How Commodore Dexter's thin old lip would have curled with contempt.

We had kept a small boat hidden in the brush. With the two black men rowing, the small craft leaped forward toward the western tip of the island.

My first sight of the *Voodoo Belle* was her high gaff sails glowing in the fire glare. Mongo Jack, as I had guessed, was taking the schooner out into Grosse Bay, and crowding on all sail as he swung for open water.

The oars bent as the Negroes pulled furiously. We cleared the island point, and saw the schooner heeling and bearing toward us like a white-winged bird rushing through the moonlight. Gouts of red flame burst from her gun ports. The roar of six-pounders rolled across the water.

Cannister was bursting on the island. I could hear the fainter reports of muskets from the undergrowth. Flames leaped on the shore, among palmetto storage sheds.

A warning shout came from the schooner's bow, as our small boat angled across her course.

"Passengers!" I shouted through cupped hands. "Captain Walker! I'm coming aboard!"

Our boat drove recklessly to the *Voodoo Belle*'s side. As I caught at the schooner's rail an unrolling rope ladder almost knocked me down. I swarmed up the ladder, followed by Sam.

"Sah, Jimbo go swamp!" he said. When I looked back over the rail the small boat was dropping astern. I knew Jimbo was swamp rat enough to go back to Crooked Bayou.

Cases of freight were stacked on the *Voodoo Belle*'s deck, and men, strange men, crowded around me. Mongo Jack pushed his way through.

"Mister Morgan! Blast me if I know what'll happen next!"

"I'll talk in your cabin, Captain. Is Irish O'Malley aboard?"

"Not he. I've been wishin' he was."

The small cabin looked luxurious after the swamp country. "A glass of Madeira?" Mongo Jack asked, grinning. "Ye look a little pale."

"Damn your Madeira!" I said. "Those were Army troops from New Orleans. They almost caught you taking aboard contraband for Mexico, didn't they?"

"We was loaded. All they found was fire in them old sheds," Mongo chortled. "For all they know, we stopped to pick up passengers or take on water. We'll strut the levee in New Orleans safe as any general, when we get back." He fingered his curly beard. "Unless," he added, "the lady hangs us. I ain't sure about the lady."

"What lady?"

"Found her stowed away when we cleared the river," said Mongo Jack. "I'll fetch her."

Mongo Jack's grinning deference was mocking as he bowed Treva Dexter into my presence.

Treva was pale and her voice was cold. "He locked me in my cabin. At your order, I suppose, Cass."

"I gave no orders," I said. "Treva, why did you do this?"

"To see if things I'd heard were true. I wanted to know if I'd nursed back to life a man who would turn against his country as soon as he was well."

"You've been listening to David Key."

"Yes," said Treva. "David said you would hang, and now I believe him."

I turned to Mongo. "Throw that contraband overboard," I ordered. "We're putting back."

Mongo Jack sneered. "O'Malley gave me orders, and they stands."

I hit him in the curly beard, and he staggered. But a blow or two never stopped a man like Mongo Jack. He bellowed—"I'm captain on me own deck!"—and rushed at me, swinging his fists.

I forgot Treva, everything but my fury, as I knocked him back on his heels. He knew every trick of foul fighting, but so did I. His big fists sledged at my chest and smashed my nose. I caught his beard and almost tore it out as I twisted his head, yanked him off balance, and hit him a thundering blow on the ear that sent him reeling.

Then, just as I was going to finish him, a pistol shot roared and my left arm went numb.

I just had time to see Jan Spreck lurching across the cabin, a pistol in each hand, when Mongo knocked me down.

The cabin blurred. I heard Treva cry: "You can't kill him!"

"Git in your cabin!" Mongo's furious, panting voice told her. "And you put the pistols up, Spreck. Let O'Malley kill his partner, if need be."

"Foolishness," Spreck told him. "He brought those soldiers to Isle Grosse."

Mongo searched me carefully and found the oiled-silk packet. He opened it under the hanging brass lantern, looked at it, then gave the paper to Spreck, who read it aloud: " 'Mister Morgan is proceeding on matters of interest to the undersigned. You will oblige, Dexter, U.S.N.' "

Spreck laughed and put the paper carefully inside his coat. "Now," he said, "we haf the Navy protecting us. Nice, no?"

I was put in irons by two seamen Mongo Jack

summoned and was shut in the storeroom. I sat in blackness, with slave shackles on ankles and wrists, and thought things out.

This, then, was what O'Malley had been holding from me. He'd known I'd not agree. The plan was perfect. Boats belonging to O'Malley and me could load contraband at Isle Grosse on their way to the Río Grande, and land the extra cargo on the Mexican coast before going on with Taylor's supplies.

No wonder Spreck and MacIntosh and Granville Crosby had wanted my friendship in Havana. The profit must be enormous. They were all in on it, working out of Cuba, getting rich by sending death to American volunteers. And I was a part of it—I, Cass Morgan, who had been a midshipman in the battle line.

Mongo Jack sent me food and water and attended to my comfort in a way. But days passed, and he left me with the rats and the dark, and the sound of sea against the *Voodoo Belle*.

I was sleeping when the schooner made her landfall and let go the anchor. Alert, I heard the sounds of small boats alongside, and cargo going over. It was easy to visualize the boats rushing contraband to some isolated spot on the Mexican coast. Hours later we sailed again.

Near noon the next day Mongo Jack had me brought to his cabin. "You'll take the Dutchman's bunk," he said. "I'll leave them shackles on your wrists, but you and me and Holly will be all cozy and comfortable, eh?"

"Where's Miss Dexter?" I asked.

"She went ashore with the Dutchman."

"You let that fat killer take her into Mexico?"

"Ain't every man has a commodore's kin to sweeten the game he's playing," Mongo assured me, grinning. "That Spreck is a deep one, if you ask me."

His backward jump was too late. I was on him, shackled wrists uplifted, and I struck down with a fury I had never known before.

The rough iron shackle bolt and the heavy lock caught Mongo under the eye and tore open his face. He dropped like a dead man. I had his keys in a moment and was at the arms chest. Pistols were always loaded and ready under the lid.

"Holly!" I roared.

The mate came down out of the sunlight, blinking. "Cap'n?"

"Come here!"

Holly saw the pistol and Mongo flat and bleeding. He snatched off his cap. "At your service, Mister Morgan, sir. You'll mind I'm only mate. I takes me orders."

"Put your middle against the pistol and unlock these shackles. Then put them on Mongo. Where's the black man who came aboard with me?"

"Ironed fo'ard."

"Get him. If there's any trouble with the crew, you'll suffer. And get a boat over with water and a few biscuits."

"Aye, aye, sir."

Mongo Jack stirred, groaning. I hauled him up and shook him.

"Where did you unload last night?"

"Mutiny!" he shouted thickly. "Holly! All hands . . ." He broke off as I cocked the pistol.

"I'd as soon shoot as not," I said. "And now, can we put back and find Miss Dexter?"

He licked his bloody mouth. "There's only an empty beach there. And like as not a Yankee gunboat looking around."

An empty beach on the wild and lonely coast of Mexico. And Jan Spreck. I thought of Treva, and every feeling I had cried out to follow her, find her, protect her. But this was war with Mexico. I'd probably fail, and I knew Treva's spirit, her fierce loyalty to country, well enough to be sure of what she would want me to do. I could hear her now, reminding me that this was war and we were Navy, that our duty was not to ourselves, to our own safety, but was where the tall masts sailed and the quarterdeck orders directed. And she was right.

I turned on Mongo Jack. "Damn you! On deck, you dirty scoundrel!"

"You'll not shoot me?" His voice showed fear.

"I'll give you an open boat, or choice of being

handed over to the Navy at Brazos de Santiago anchorage, off the Río Grande."

"The Navy'll hang me!"

"Too good for you. Take the open boat. And if you find Jan Spreck, warn him that if Miss Dexter is harmed, I'll kill him if I have to follow him all over the earth!"

"An open boat is murder!" Mongo protested, and began to curse. He was still cursing as he drifted astern in the boat. Actually, he'd not have too much trouble making the coast if the wind held fair.

I had Holly lay the crew aft, and I looked them over. They were sweepings of the Caribbean, including the eight men taken aboard at Isle Grosse.

"You'll hang for that little business at Isle Grosse," I told them, a pistol in each hand. "By now every Navy hull west of the Mississippi will be looking for this schooner. I'm going to try and make Cuba. If there's any among you with other ideas, Sam, here, will be watching beside me while I sleep. I warn you. . . . Now get forward and work smartly. We'll change our paint and name. Pirates or traitors, we'll all hang no higher."

V

My pride had gone. Shame and anger were with me in those days we ran toward Cuba. I had slight feeling about David Key. He had faded into the shifting fortunes of war. But the thought of Treva stayed with me like the ache of a hurt beyond healing.

"What are you, Cass Morgan?" the commodore had asked me in Havana.

He had his answer. Scum. Smuggler. Gunrunner. Traitor. The very letter he had given me was being used against the fleet. As the tall mainmast swept against the stars on the run east, the commodore stayed in my thoughts.

I drove the crew, ate little, and slept less. I had changed the *Voodoo Belle*'s name to the *Amanda*, and painted the hull white with black trimmings. Mongo Jack had carried extra papers. All of our boats did. We had traded and run cargo in vague and devious ways, and we were always prepared.

It hurt to have that powder cargo for General Taylor broken out and heaved over, but it had to go. The schooner was a deathtrap in a fight, with powder stowed below.

I wanted Granville Crosby, and MacIntosh, and Irish O'Malley, if he'd escaped from New Orleans. So I went to Havana, knowing the cowed crew would not run the risk of hang ropes, by talking.

We sailed in past the Morro boldly. My false papers passed the port officials, and I made sure of it with a discreet passage of money.

I was wondering how to get ashore, whether I could trust Holly and the crew with the schooner, when a boat came alongside, and a man, a little older than I, with a great flaming red beard, swung aboard. It was Captain Johnny Frink. He punched me in the ribs and winked.

"I seen you pass the Morro," he said. "*Amanda*, eh? Ain't this the *Voodoo Belle*? What slippery business are you and O'Malley up to now?"

"Have you seen O'Malley?" I asked as we went below. "Is he in Havana?"

"I've not seen him," said Johnny Frink. "I've been too busy celebrating good fortune." His deep laugh filled the cabin. "Nigh three hundred pieces of good fortune. Over the beach and inland without a hitch."

"Slaves again? You'll sweat for it someday, Johnny," I warned.

"Fine talk," said Johnny. "At least I'll never carry powder and shot to anyone who'll fire them back at American boys."

"There's a meaning behind that remark," I suggested, not smiling.

Johnny Frink nodded. "Cap'n Juniper Woods is in the harbor now. The brig *Balmoye*. Off

Yucatan Strait, Cap'n Woods spoke a schooner on a southbound course. He got no reply. Through the glass, he was sure he saw O'Malley by the mainmast. O'Malley knew well enough who was master of the *Balmoye*."

Johnny uncorked a wine bottle with his teeth, drank deeply, and looked at me. "And I," he said, "know bloody well what's going on. O'Malley was nigh caught in New Orleans. It's a dirty business, bucko."

"So O'Malley went south, through the Yucatan Strait?" I said, and drank, too. "Maybe you'd like to help stop it, Johnny?"

"Maybe I would."

"Will you?" I asked. "It's a dirtier business to me than it is to you. I've broken with O'Malley, whether he knows it or not."

I knew by his narrowed eyes that Johnny was weighing me and each word.

"I've made money and not been proud of some of it," he said. "A little glory in stopping blockade-running against our troops wouldn't be amiss. It might make me hold my head a little higher when I walk across Boston Common to see my old mother."

I knew he would do it, and I told him all that had happened.

"You see how it is, Johnny? The din lot of them have to be brought in . . . O'Malley, Crosby, and the rest. I've got to do it. I know their tricks. I

171

was blind and let it happen, and now I've got to stop it."

"By God, Cass, I'm with you!"

"This schooner will do."

"Back your sails," warned Johnny. "There's a pile of planning. More guns. The right crew. O'Malley ain't a man to trifle with. Nor the others."

Johnny sent for some of his crew to come aboard and watch the schooner, and before dark I went ashore, to Papa Pio's place.

Granville Crosby, I found, was not in Havana. A carriage bore me to the house of Ramón Rodriguez, the elegant and shady Havana lawyer. It was the social hour, but Rodriguez welcomed me into his study. He had my health in his fine brandy, and he held a candle to my cigar.

"I have heard from New Orleans," he informed me. "There has been trouble, *señor*? Ah, yes. I place myself at your service."

I wondered how much at my service and tested him with a question. "Where can I find Granville Crosby?"

Rodriguez lifted thin black eyebrows. "I have heard that *Señor* Crosby has been in Jamaica. If not . . ." He shrugged.

"Then you can't help me at all?"

He spread slender hands regretful and changed the subject.

"Have you seen, *señor*, our gifted and beautiful friend, *Señorita* Valverde?"

"Yes. In New Orleans, and very much the toast of Royal Street."

Rodriguez smiled. "In Havana now, *señor*," he corrected. "She will sail tomorrow on an English boat for Veracruz and Mexico City. Art," he observed, "is above war."

As soon as possible, I left. It was strange how desperately I felt about seeing Susanne before she vanished into Mexico.

Susanne showed no great surprise when I arrived at her door. Her welcome was calm, casual. Only in me, it seemed, was the explosive past between us as I took her hand.

I rebelled against this new Susanne, this indifference she could not really feel. She could not have forgotten those moments in the quiet patio.

"Sit down, Cass." Susanne smiled. "And don't look so stern, so fierce."

She sat beside me, slender, graceful as always. "I know, why you did not return to New Orleans," she said slowly. "No, please listen, Cass."

She reached for my hand. My pulse began to race, and then subsided. Her touch was as calm as her manner. Something had gone from between us.

"We're so much alike," Susanne said. "All the world is ours for the taking, and we reach for it. I

173

think I loved you, Cass. I think I still love you. . . . No, don't! Listen to me." She moved away.

"You're acting very strangely, Susanne."

"I know you. I know you so well, Cass, because I know myself. So I must tell you. Between us I will not have thoughts that are not spoken. You see what love means to me?"

"I'd never have thought it meant acting like a sister."

She looked at me. Her mouth was tender, but her eyes looked sad.

"I have danced in many countries," she said slowly. "But I have only one country, Cass." Her hand tightened on mine. "I'd not do anything to hurt my country or my people."

She made me think of Treva Dexter. The same fierce pride in flag and country. I had thought them different. A world apart. Treva lovely, proud. Susanne all fire and passion and recklessness. To each some part of me had reached out. Now, suddenly, I was uncertain.

"So we're not alike, after all?" I said.

"I begged you to be careful," Susanne reminded me.

"Did you know that Granville Crosby, Jan Spreck, and the others were dealing with Mexico?"

"Yes."

"I was a fool. I didn't suspect, until it was too late. Not even when they tried to kill me, so I'd

174

not influence O'Malley. He didn't tell me our boats were smuggling contraband through the blockade." I stood up. "I tried to stop it, and I was too late."

"Oh, Cass! I should have known! I'm a fool!" Susanne came to me blindly, eyes filling. She put her cheek against my chest and held me a moment. And then she stepped back, smiling, blinking. "Tell me, Cass."

So while we stood at the tall windows, arms about each other, Susanne's head against my shoulder, I told her all that had happened.

"Spreck took Treva Dexter into Mexico," I said. "He'll see Treva is made useful to their plans." I took a deep breath. "Susanne, you'll have the run of Mexico. Will you find Treva and keep her safe?"

I felt her stiffen against me.

"I hate her," she said abruptly. "In New Orleans I met this Captain Key. Yes, after I heard what had happened at Isle Grosse, I had to see him. He told me about this girl. He told me how you had turned her head years ago, and then again in New Orleans. You could not stay away from her in New Orleans. He thinks you have taken her away for yourself."

"Ridiculous! I was helpless."

"But you still want her. And I hate her!" Susanne burst out with passion. "You're frantic with worry about her."

"It's my fault she's where she is."

Susanne laughed scornfully. "Your fault? Who asked her aboard your schooner? Oh, Cass! I'm not quarreling. I'm not even jealous. Don't look at me like that. I just hate her." Then she turned to me, inside the circle of my arm. "But if you want her, Cass, I'll find her. Hold me just once, and don't say anything, before I go into Mexico and find her for you."

I said huskily: "Never another like you, Susanne." I kissed the sweetness of her hair, and held her closer, and put a hand under her chin and brought her face up. Her eyes were closed.

"Don't, Cass. Not when she's between us. Not when I must find her for you to hold. . . ."

I kissed the words away, and felt fire run wild through me again, and through Susanne. I caught her up lightly and swung to the couch where we had sat, and paused a moment, kissing her eyelids, her cheeks, and then the softness of her mouth, fiercely. Then I knelt and put her gently down and held her close.

She protested, and then clung and held me. She knew; I knew. So much alike. Wildness in each of us that met wildness until we were exhausted. And when she lay gasping against me, her hand touched my cheek. Eyes closed, she murmured that sweetest, tenderest word of all Spanish. "*Querido* . . . beloved. *Querido mio, te amo* . . . I love you."

176

The next morning I saw Susanne off in a harbor boat to the British steamer *Falcon*. Then I forced myself to stop thinking about her, and went to see Johnny Frink.

Johnny's schooner, the *Scudder*, carried carronades and a long-gun. We took those for the *Amanda* and purchased four more brass carronades of six-pounder size.

"If we have trouble, we'll close in," I said. "Leave long-guns and solid shot for Navy gunners. We'll do better with langrage and cannister and chain-shot."

Johnny culled men from the *Scudder*. We combed the waterfront for more good hands. Then, at the last minute, I sent Holly and most of the old crew ashore for a drunk, with their full pay, and we brought the new crew aboard and sailed.

Salty old Navy gunners had taught me gunnery. I formed gun crews and drilled them hard in the way of running out, firing, reloading, before they dashed across deck to serve the other guns. I drilled them with boarding nets, cutlass work, and fast and steady musket fire. Navy style.

We sailed south into the Caribbean. "They must have a base this way, if O'Malley was sighted on his course," I told Johnny Frink. "And it can't be far south of Yucatan Strait."

We made landfall at Espiritu Santo Bay, and

found nothing. We sailed northward again for Cozumel Island, some ten miles off the mainland.

From the masthead I trained a long-glass on sandy beaches and rocky points, and over the low tree-studded island. There was no sign that boats had used the place for a base.

We took the *Amanda* offshore for the night. Restlessness sent me to the masthead again, where stars and moon drenched light over an empty world.

There, later in the night, I sighted a distant sail bearing across our course.

"Sail ho-o-o!" I called down.

Johnny Frink was waiting when I reached the deck. "Running in toward Cozumel, or the mainland, north of the island," I said. "Running in under cover of the night. She sighted us and started about. Lay alongside her. She's ours!"

"Piracy, if we fire on her and are wrong," Johnny reminded me.

"Worse, if we're right and lose her," I said sharply.

Johnny shouted for all hands, and all sail. I went to my guns.

VI

We had the wind and the shorter leg of that run out to sea through the moonlight. "She's guilty, or she'd not be running," I told Johnny.

By this time sand and water, powder and chain-shot, langrage, swabs, and rammers, all the gear of gunnery were out and ready. I had served out muskets, cutlasses, and pistols. Netting was up, against any try to board us. All the tedious drilling of the crew was bearing fruit.

I ordered chain and langrage into starboard and larboard carronades, and chain-shot in the swivel gun. If that fleeing schooner expected ball to be lobbed wildly around her, she was due for a surprise.

The cook set out hot food and strong coffee, and as the night hours wore away, we came up slowly on the strange schooner. I was sighting the long-gun myself, when the screeching howl of a ball came at us out of the night. The shot struck short, came off the water, and crashed against the *Amanda*'s hull.

"Steady!" I called. "We've an answer for that!"

The *Amanda* shook as the long-gun went off, double-shotted with chain. When the flash cleared out of our eyes, the other craft's foresail was split and her gaff was hanging down.

"Close in!" I shouted to Frink.

Side carronades fired at us. A hail of iron langrage struck us. A man screamed with pain. Some of the light rigging was severed, and then the *Amanda* heeled and shook as starboard carronades fired in battery.

Sails slatted. The booms swept over. In a din of shouted orders, the men jumped to their duties. The larboard guns came to bear, and I called the order to fire.

It was a full strike the length of the stranger's deck, taffrail forward. She was a tangle of ruined gear and shredded canvas as Johnny came about again and ran up under her stern. His voice boomed out through the speaking trumpet.

"What boat? Where bound?"

"*Dolphin*! Mobile to Kingston! Cap'n Sanford! What the devil kind of piracy is this?"

I ran to Johnny and the trumpet. On all the oceans there could be only one outraged bellow like that.

"O'Malley!" I roared through the trumpet. "I'm boarding you! Cass Morgan!"

No one but O'Malley would have answered in such a jeering humor, with blood and treason and death between us. "Come aboard and I'll open a bottle, Cass! I've been expecting you!"

"Just like O'Malley to try and talk himself out of it," said Johnny.

"He's tricky," I warned. "Dangerous when he talks most. Watch him."

Johnny brought us in close, recklessly, through the first cool dawn, and the *Dolphin*'s guns caught us full, without warning. The *Amanda* shuddered mortally from the hell of metal that struck her water line. A flying wood splinter laid open my cheek.

"Aim at her deck!" I shouted. "Then all hands for boarding!"

I doubt if O'Malley expected the fearful mass of langrage, nails, old bolts, and chunks of scrap iron that our carronades blasted across his deck. There were wild shouts and cries of pain on the *Dolphin* as Johnny Frink brought us hull to hull with a grinding shock.

Our men raised a shout as they followed me over with cutlasses and pistols. Wilson, a long-necked man, was a leader, despite a bloody and almost useless leg. Aldie, our slow-speaking bosun, had become a demon, with a cutlass in each hand and a dirk hanging behind his neck.

While the two crews mixed in a mad mêlée, I found O'Malley waiting for me.

"I knew ye'd come!" he shouted. He hurled a cutlass, point down, into the deck and beckoned with a huge paw. "Will you fight fair?"

I covered him with a cocked pistol. "You've had your fight and fun, Irish! Get to the cabin!"

"What!" he bawled in astonishment. "You'll not fight?"

"I'll blow your head off, you tricky, black-hearted Irishman! But you'll not have the fun of fighting for it. Get to the cabin!"

He was almost sheepish as he stalked below. I caught a last blurred glimpse of the *Amanda* drifting away, her mainmast canted drunkenly, one rail under. Then I faced O'Malley in the cabin, with the uproar of fighting still above us.

His dark-burned face was a study in angry uncertainty. "What do you mean to do, Cass? Hang me?"

"You fool," I said. "You should be hung. After all our years together. After all we had ahead of us, you smash everything like a greedy, treacherous idiot!"

O'Malley winced. "I didn't mean it that way, Cass. It didn't seem so bad at first. A little trick, like, to make a mountain of money, while still helping out with the war. More of a joke."

"War," I said angrily, "is no joke. A sniveling midshipman would have known better. You've made a traitor out of me. We're both going to pay. Now what do you know about Treva Dexter?"

"Nothing," said O'Malley, cast down. "I never was one of them. Their plans were no concern of mine."

"You stayed with them."

"Nothing else to do. That Captain Key came back from Isle Grosse and almost had me by the heels before I slipped out of New Orleans. The Navy gobbled all our boats quick. I thought best to keep away from Havana."

Johnny Frink came bursting into the cabin, waving a pistol. "We've got a gent named Crosby, and one called Macintosh."

"Bring 'em in, boys."

Crosby and Macintosh were herded in at pistol's point. Crosby's fine linen was rumpled, his thin face haggard. The square and pious face of Macintosh looked as if it had finally met the devil and a fearful reckoning.

"Gentlemen," I said, "it's going to be a pleasure to put you in irons. Where is Jan Spreck?"

Macintosh muttered that Spreck was in Mexico. Crosby tried to be suave and argue of profits if I would listen. I ordered them into slave shackles below deck, and had O'Malley shackled, too. But I let him stay in the cabin.

The *Amanda* had gone down. Johnny Frink was cheerful. "We've still got a boat to sail, Cass. What now?"

"This is Navy business," I said. "They'll have to know."

"They want you, too, Cass."

"I'm finished with running away."

"As you will. It's you who will suffer when the Navy lays hands on you."

"At least," I said, "I'll have my self-respect. I've done what had to be done."

We sailed the *Dolphin* north through Yucatan Strait, repairing battle damage, bending fresh canvas, doctoring the wounded. Irish O'Malley, with only wrist shackles, had the run of the deck.

When the day came to face the Navy, there was irony in it for me. We were on course for the Mississippi when we sighted a Navy sloop, just out of the river. I put her in the glass. "She looks like the *Vandoria*!" I exclaimed.

She was the *Vandoria*. In an hour she became aware we were closing for a purpose, and shortened sail, and let us come up.

I hailed her. "Is Lieutenant Peters aboard?"

"Lieutenant Peters commanding! Is that Mister Morgan?"

"Coming aboard!"

Johnny Frink shook my hand as I went over the rail. "Luck, Cass."

"I'll need it."

Jock Peters met me as I stepped on his deck. His round face was sober.

"Orders are out to take you on sight, Cass," he informed me formally. "Consider yourself a prisoner, sir. Is that your schooner?"

"Whatever you care to make her, Jock. And remember, I had to chase you, to surrender."

Jock coughed and masked a smile. In his cramped cabin, he exploded: "Damn, Cass! I'd rather do anything than this. Here I've my own command at last, and one of my first duties is this sorry business with an old shipmate."

"I'll explain," I said, and Jock listened, clearing his throat now and then. He opened a bottle, and put a glass in my hand, and sipped his own wine, while he watched my face.

"I want word sent quickly to Commodore Dexter about all this," I said when I'd finished my story.

Jock smiled. "Might be done. I'm carrying urgent dispatches, and some are for Commodore Dexter, at Isle Lobos. I'll put my junior lieutenant in charge of your schooner, and we'll all go there and let the commodore ponder what next. Meanwhile, mister, act like a proper prisoner, or your bottles will be empty."

"Jock," I said, and had to try again. "Why, damn you, Jock. . . ."

So I came back to the Navy, even if a prisoner. I was not eager to face that thin old man we would find at Isle Lobos. But it had to be done.

VII

It was late in February when we raised the island. The *Dolphin*, sailing close, followed our lead toward anchorage behind a bold reef that extended southeasterly from the island.

Jock, was as much astonished as I at what we saw. "God's favor, Cass. All the ships in the Gulf must be here. Look at them! Frigates, steamers, transports, brigs, schooners. There's nigh a hundred, if there's one. Something big is brewing."

Anchorage behind the south reef offered good shelter. Once I had put in here with my *Blue Turk* schooner. Isle Lobos then had been covered with wild trees and shrubs. Now the whole small island was a teeming Army camp. The banyan trees, the wild lemon and lime trees, the palms and tangled vines, had been thinned out. Tents stood in orderly rows. Soldiers moved everywhere.

We were hailed by a steam tug. A pilot came aboard and took us inside the reef. Jock had donned his best uniform. He put off in his gig with the dispatches.

My midshipman years were very close as I stood on Jock's spotless deck and watched the armada of shipping gathered about. Navy discipline and smartness were everywhere. Navy might, Navy pride, towered there in the great frigates.

I was not a part of it. I was Cass Morgan, prisoner. But I was proud. My heart stirred faster. My throat tightened.

Jock returned. He was hurried. "The commodore will see you. My gig will take you, without irons, to the frigate *Peloneon*, where he is in quarters."

"What did he say, Jock?"

"Little enough. He's a cold one. I risked speaking my best for you, Cass. He made no comment. Are you ready?"

As the gig approached the *Peloneon*, the frigate's great masts and yards gleamed in the sunlight. The black snouts of her cannon bristled through her open gun ports. The crew was busy as Jock was piped aboard.

Once I, too, could have been a part of the stiff saluting that followed. The deck officer was rigidly correct to Jock.

"Prisoner to the quarterdeck," he ordered.

Jock, to his relief, I was sure, was turned loose aboard, to await the commodore's pleasure. Two ramrod-like marines hustled me aft. The awful majesty of a commodore, on a frigate's sacred quarterdeck, received me. Here, the dry little man I had talked to in Papa Pio's dim back room became God Almighty. He was majesty supreme, life, destiny, to all the gold braid and all the seamen under him. You forgot his size; you saw the gold braid on his uniform; you felt the frosty stab of his look.

That look was on me now, as he turned from the rail. "I'll see you in my cabin," he said coldly.

At least he plucked me from the haughty marines. He walked stiffly ahead of me to that most sacred holy of holies, where not even the frigate's commander stepped without invitation.

The massive deck beams were low overhead, the space was cramped, but this was awesome territory. There was an awesome note in the brief and icy question Commodore Dexter asked me when the door was closed.

"Where is my granddaughter?"

"You've had no word of her, sir?"

"Yes," he said. "One letter, sent out of Mexico in the British mails. It warned me that Treva's life depended on my honoring the pass I gave you."

My heart sank. "Did you do anything about the pass, sir?"

"I had already taken measures," said Commodore Dexter coldly. "My orders were given to bring in anyone found with that pass. There have been reports that it was used twice before my order got around to all commanders. I have been reprimanded for being so careless as to issue such a paper." His eyes flashed fire. "At my age, with the record I've made, I was reprimanded. Thanks to you."

He turned to his cabin window and looked out. A trace of huskiness was in his voice when next he spoke.

"I loved my granddaughter. She resembled my wife, who died when Treva's mother was born."

I'd rather he had ordered me to the gratings to be flogged. "Would you care to hear what happened, sir?"

"Mister Peters gave me your version. Eloquently." He turned, indifferent again.

"I would have followed Treva into Mexico," I said, "but Spreck had her a full day or two ahead of me. A Yankee, like myself, could not have gotten far into Mexico in these times. And then, there was more than Treva, too."

"What?"

"Your pass, sir. Spreck had it. I knew the Navy would take steps to void it. It seemed more important to go about the business of stopping the blockade-running."

"Indeed?" he said. "You were getting rich, I believe. Matters of your own to worry about."

"Even a rascal has a country," I told him. "I was a midshipman once. I found I couldn't forget it. I've done all I could. I've surrendered, to pay the fiddler."

"Ah," said the frosty old man, "there's always a payment to the fiddler. You're sorry, eh? You'd like a little mercy? After all, you did bring in a prize, and some of the precious rascals who were breaking our blockade."

"Sir," I said, stung at last, "confound your mercy. If my neck were worrying me, I'd have gone in another direction with the *Dolphin*."

"I don't believe I understand your reasoning," he remarked dryly.

"I think you do, sir. Else why did you trust me with that pass?" And while he watched me without expression, I said: "Treva had no business leaving New Orleans. Men are dying in this war. Even loving Treva, I had to go on to stop the dirty business I'd been tricked into. And let her safety wait a bit." I looked him in the eye. "If I hadn't, she would have less use for me than she has now."

"I see you know Treva," he said gravely. "What have you to suggest about her, and this man Spreck?"

"Treva may be safe," I said slowly. I told him of Susanne Valverde's promise, in Havana, before Susanne sailed for Mexico. "On the other hand," I said, "Treva may be in danger. Granville Crosby warned me that if harm came to him or Macintosh, Treva would suffer. Jan Spreck will stop at nothing."

"Ah," he said. "Of course. We must expect that. Now, sir, would you care to give me your parole?"

My smile was bitter. "Hadn't you better ask that of an officer and a gentleman, sir? Aren't you forgetting who I am?"

"Why, no," he said evenly, "I know quite well who you are. Might I suggest you be good enough to give your parole, for all circumstances which may be suggested?"

I had to swallow hard. "I give you my parole, sir, in whatever form you choose to say."

"Very good." He studied me thoughtfully. "We are sailing to take Veracruz by bombardment and storm," he said. "General Scott is in command of the troops. Approaching battle is always friendly to lawless men, Mister Morgan. Men like this Jan Spreck are at their worst." He pulled his lip. "I can put you ashore at Veracruz. The rest would be up to you."

He opened a locker drawer and took out a newspaper, the worse for wear.

"This was brought aboard by a visiting Englishman, straight from Mexico City. Your speaking of the dancer reminded me that she was mentioned in this paper. She was dancing in Mexico City then, but the account says, I believe, that she intended going to Veracruz for an engagement. If you go ashore . . ."

"I'll report back, sir, if alive," I said eagerly.

"Good."

"May I speak for Irish O'Malley, sir?"

"He will have his chance to speak for himself." The commodore returned to brusqueness. "Report to the officer at the gangway. I'll request the captain to provide you space until we're off Veracruz."

He barely nodded when I thanked him. But I left his cabin a new man. My parole had been considered worth taking by a flag officer of the fleet. Only a man parted from pride, lost in deep and bitter shame, could have known what that meant.

VIII

I was told twelve thousand soldiers were aboard the transports that sailed from Isle Lobos. The tall white sails, the flags, pennants, the trailing smoke plumes from the fast steamers seemed to blanket the sea.

A cold norther struck and was still blowing when the fleet sighted the blockade squadron at Veracruz, and sailed into Anton Lizardo anchorage, south of the city.

The next day we saw the snow peak of Orizabo, inland. The following day word passed from ship to ship that General Scott was on the steamer *Petrita*, with Commodore Conner, reconnoitering the Veracruz approaches. Tension mounted.

Hills of loose sand, dense chaparral surrounded

the massive walls of Veracruz. Unhealthy swamps lay behind the city.

The defenses were formidable. The Veracruz guns were backed by the great batteries of San Juan de Ulúa, the almost impregnable fortress on a rocky island just offshore. I was still aboard the *Peloneon* when the landing started and could watch the tremendous spectacle.

This was history. A hundred years from this March day of 1847, when all the world, God pray, would be peaceful, prosperous, knowing little of war, men would read about this mightiest force any country had ever put ashore against an enemy.

The cold norther had blown out. The sea was calm, its depths clear. The sun poured dazzling light.

Before noon the steamer *Princeton* led off anchorage, towing the *Raritan*. The steamer *Massachusetts* moved next, carrying General Scott and his staff. Everywhere one looked the brilliant sunlight was flashing off sharp, fixed bayonets.

Under easy sail the rest of the ships moved, towing big surf boats which would carry the troops ashore. In the rear of the American armada were warships of European nations, their decks, masts, rigging crowded with spectators.

In the middle of the afternoon the warships and transports anchored opposite Sacrificios Island, each ship in its assigned position. The huge surf boats, each holding a hundred men, took position at the ships' gangways.

By four o'clock, four thousand five hundred men were in the surf boats, which extended abreast in a solid, mile-long line. A midshipman excitedly told me the boats held General Worth's division, given the honor of landing first.

The deep, somber report of a signal gun came from the *Massachusetts*. Cheers went up from all the fleet. Bands burst into martial music on all sides. The surf boats started toward the shore.

The great guns of San Juan de Ulúa, to the north, opened up. We could see shells bursting and round shot skipping on water and shore. But, strangely, the gray, threatening walls of Veracruz were silent. Not a gun was fired from the city as the soldiers leaped waist-deep into beach water and dashed ashore.

The flag went up as the sun was setting. The flag—on enemy territory. It was rippling in the breeze as darkness fell and the surf boats returned to load again. By ten o'clock that night twelve thousand men were ashore.

The sun came up in a blaze next morning, and the batteries of Veracruz and San Juan de Ulúa opened with full fury. The fleet guns began to answer. From then on during the siege, the din of gunfire and crash of exploding shells was continuous, save when the wind blew sand so thick men on shore were all but blinded.

I wondered if Susanne Valverde and Treva Dexter could be behind those grim walls of Veracruz, where already shells were bursting, and toward which all hell would shortly be loosed from our shore batteries. Curiously, at a time when I should have been thinking solely of Treva's safety, the thought of Susanne's danger tortured my imagination just as much. I wondered if I would live to get inside the city and search for them.

A young midshipman finally sought me out the next morning, with word that the commodore wished to see me.

In his quarters, Commodore Dexter spoke briskly. "I've been waiting for word from inside the city. General Scott has ways of hearing things. Now I can tell you that your dancer was in Veracruz three days ago, entertaining for the garrison and population in a small makeshift theater, just off the main plaza. There is still time for you to enter the city before investment is complete, if your wits are sharp enough. Have you any plans?"

"I'll make my plans, sir, to suit the cut of the moment."

He nodded. "The best I can do for you is another pass, good inside our Army lines. You run the risk of being shot as a spy, of course, if caught in Veracruz."

"Yes, sir."

He gave me the pass. "We're sending shells ashore in an hour. Go in the first boat. What kind of arms will you want?"

"I have a knife, sir. It'll do for the present."

He said—"Good luck."—and drew a long breath. "Tell Treva the same, from me, young man."

"Yes, sir, when and where I find her, Veracruz or inland."

He nodded again, and I left him with that understanding; wherever Treva was, I'd find her, no matter how long it took. And Susanne. And then I'd be back to pay the fiddler for O'Malley's recklessness and my blindness.

A deeply loaded surf boat put me on the beach. I struck inland, asking questions as I went.

General Worth's men were on the right of the line, nearest the city. Gideon Pillow, with Tennessee and Pennsylvania regiments, had advanced to an old building at the head of the Laguna Malibrah, and was pressing forward toward the road connecting Veracruz with the small village of Medellin, south down the coast a few miles. Scattered Mexican forces were retreating to the shelter of the city guns.

It took many questions and much footwork before I advanced far enough to know all that. There was furious activity everywhere. Heavy guns, ammunition, supplies were being laboriously advanced through the high hills of loose sand.

The landscape was broken, rugged. Roads had to be cut through the dense chaparral. And always, in the background, were the deep reports of fleet and fortress guns and exploding shells.

Every man who moved was burdened with his provisions and arms. The enemy was striking repeatedly at various parts of the front line. Now here, now there, with storms of musket fire, quick retreats, sharp advances at another spot.

Men were fighting and dying and laboring mightily, as the siege ring was slowly, stubbornly stretched about the defiant walled city. Wounded men with bloody bandages were straggling back through the chaparral.

"What's ahead?" I asked one unshaven man from a Tennessee regiment.

He spat tobacco juice and grinned wearily at me. "Hit ain't no turkey shoot, mister. Them Mexes is full of vinegar and spit. He looked at me curiously. "You sight-seein' er what, without no gun er unyform?"

"I'm looking around," I said. "Have you seen a dead Mexican about my size?"

He looked at me and grinned thinly as he thumbed back the way he had come. "Go git you one, mister. They's all sizes fer the takin'."

Pillow's men were in the sand hills and chaparral when I found them. They were driving a Mexican force from the Medellin road toward the city. Well toward dark, shells came from the city batteries to protect the retreating enemy. Orders were passed to halt, close up, and form for the night.

It was there in light chaparral between two sand hills, just before dark, that an officer headed me off on the double with a squad of riflemen.

"Hold still, Morgan!" the officer shouted. "Don't run or you'll be shot."

And I would be shot. When David Key talked of killing me, he could be believed.

"Well, David," I said when he confronted me, "I see you reached the fighting. But do you need all the Army to back you up each time we meet?"

"Take this man!" Key ordered the soldiers. "Shoot instantly if he tries to get away. He's a traitor, wanted for hanging, back in the States. Doubtless he'll get a drumhead court and be shot here on the field."

"You needn't have me pawed over. I've no weapon but a knife," I told David Key when a corporal started to search me.

The corporal stepped back with my knife. David moved in, and spoke low, for my ear alone. "Where's Treva? What did you do to her?"

"Is this your drumhead court?"

"You know it isn't," Key said between his teeth.

"If I weren't an officer and a gentleman, I'd have shot you on sight."

"I doubt it, David. Then you couldn't have asked me about Treva." And because I was annoyed, I asked: "Do you want me dead worse than you want Treva alive?"

It was dangerous baiting. The man was almost out of his mind with hatred of me and worry about Treva.

"Where is she?" he demanded.

"She's probably in Mexico. That's all I know. Now what are you going to do?"

Key drew one of the rare Colt repeating revolvers from his holster. He was so pale that the sword mark I'd put on his cheek years ago was like a band of happy color.

"Good enough, Corporal," he said in a choked voice. "Go about your business. I'll continue with the prisoner." And to me: "Start walking to your right. I'll shoot if you even look like running."

"You're making a mistake, David."

"I'm Captain Key, sir! Walk!"

I walked, since Key's way was my way. But I was dubious. He was in a state where control might slip. My back was a tempting target.

We walked beyond General Pillow's men, and passed more dead horses and dead men, Mexican and American. I noticed a Mexican officer of dragoons who seemed to be about my size.

The sun had plunged behind the western mountains, when we were challenged by a sentry. We had reached Colonel Campbell's First Tennessee Regiment, which was holding the stone powder magazine behind the city. A guard took us to the colonel's post beside the stone building.

David saluted stiffly, produced orders, which he had been carrying, and said: "On the way here I captured a known traitor, and probably a spy, sir. He was moving about inside our lines without a uniform." He glared at me. "If I had the authority, I'd order him shot out of hand."

Colonel Campbell was dusty, even to his mustache. He looked tired, but he smiled as he folded Key's orders.

"Well, now, Captain, perhaps it's a good thing you don't have the authority. Has your prisoner admitted he was spying inside our lines?"

"No, sir. He's clever, I warn you."

The colonel walked to me. "What have you got to say for yourself, my man?" He looked me up and down. "Spying is a serious business."

"Naturally, Colonel. I was trying to find this powder magazine when Captain Key took command." I smiled. "He made a good guide. Brought me straight here." I gave him Commodore Dexter's paper.

Colonel Campbell began to chuckle as he looked at it, then handed it to Key.

"It can't be!" David gulped, as he read. "Why, the Navy wants him! He was running arms through the blockade. He's a known slaver and smuggler. A . . . a damned desperado, if there ever was one."

"He's well backed by authority," Colonel Campbell said good-naturedly. "You see, Captain, why it's a good idea not to get hot-headed about shooting? Or do you question Commodore Dexter's right to use this man on Navy business?"

"My God, no, sir!" David gulped. His face was red. "But I can't understand it. Commodore Dexter? I'd think *he'd* be the last man . . ." He broke off, glowering at me.

"Well, now that we're all agreed, what's your purpose, Mister Morgan?"

"Tonight," I said, "I'll move beyond your lines and get to the city walls."

"Hmmm. You speak Spanish?"

"Fluently," I said. "With a passable Mexican idiom. We passed a dead Mexican dragoon officer back there, Colonel. I'd like to take over his uniform and rank and see if I can't get into the city tonight. I'd like to be passed beyond your sentries."

The colonel laughed. "A Mexican uniform would be just the reason for my men to shoot. Oh, Lieutenant Cherry. Escort Mister Morgan to his new uniform, then bring him back here. I want to see how he looks."

It was dark before we located my dead officer.

The lieutenant helped me change clothes, and we returned to the stone magazine, carrying my own clothes and shoes. David Key was not about, but the colonel joined us.

He looked at me and whistled softly. "Not bad. In fact, perfect, all but that dried blood on the shoulder."

"I'll give myself a bandage for a head wound," I decided. "He was killed by a musket ball through the head."

"Anything else? What arms do you need?"

"I have this saber. Someone got his pistol. But I don't mean to fight, Colonel. A one-man battle with the Veracruz garrison won't get me far."

"I wish you luck," Colonel Campbell told me dubiously as he shook my hand. Lieutenant Cherry escorted me beyond the Tennessee regiment's line, gripped my hand, and stood there while I vanished in the night.

From that moment on I forgot Cass Morgan. I was Dragoon Lieutenant José Fernández y Montoya. The name was my own invention. My life depended on not slipping out of character for an instant.

IX

The night trembled with the bombardment of great guns from the fleet, from the city, and from the fortress of San Juan de Ulúa. Exploding shells were like heat lightning flicking across the sky. One, falling near, rattled grapeshot like hail through the dry chaparral.

A horse nickered sharply to my left. I heard a wounded man groaning, calling weakly in Spanish for water. He was on the ground, out of his head, clutching the reins of the horse with an unconscious death grip.

Mercy aside, here was luck. I rode from there with the dying man across the saddle. When the first challenge came, it was an *escopeta* shot, followed by an alarmed shout to halt.

"Mother of God!" I cried furiously in Spanish. "Are the wounded left to be killed by the cursed *Yanquis*, and then fired on when we seek safety? Lieutenant Fernández y Montoya orders you to advance and assist!"

"A thousand pardons, my lieutenant! How were we to know?"

It was an advance squad from *el Onze*, the Eleventh Regiment, posted well out from the city walls to observe American intentions through the night. The leader was a non-commissioned man, not sure where his officer could be found.

"Enough!" I cut short his ramblings. "We die while you stumble around like blind burros! I will take two men to assist us to the city gate! Your two best men!"

I proceeded on the crowbait horse with an escort afoot, while the wounded man groaned without pause.

We were challenged again and again, and I was a better Mexican than any that we met.

I came out on a road. The city guns were close ahead. The great wall loomed high. The vast gates were open. Men, horses, carts were passing in and out, many more coming out than in. The civilians of the city were escaping before the siege lines were closed. In a day or so Veracruz would be a rat trap waiting bombardment by heavy mortars and cannon.

"¡*Viva Santa Anna!*" I shouted.

My escort shouted *vivas*. The escaping mob joined in. Cheering let out their excitement, gave them hope, bolstered their defiance. And I, Lieutenant Fernández y Montoya, rode through the clamor with my head bandaged, my wounded man, and my escort. Not even a second lieutenant questioned my right to pass inside the gate.

It was done. I was in. Confusion to those rascally *Americanos*.

"Take this man to help," I ordered my escort. I gave them money I found in my uniform.

"Drink to Santa Anna before returning to battle."

Confusion was on all sides. Now and then a shell from the fleet burst among the buildings with a muffled roar. Screams and cries, snatches of prayer, furious oaths greeted each explosion.

I rode through the bedlam, without trouble, head bandaged, more war-like than Santa Anna himself in my scarlet uniform. I wanted to find out if Susanne Valverde had been dancing in the city, and where she might now be.

The place for all that and other gossip was the *fonda*, the inn, of *Monsieur* Forbat, a Frenchman, just off the great plaza. I was just turning the corner to go there when the cry of "¡*Muerte al Americano*!" reached me.

For an instant I thought the shout was for me. But bobbing lanterns to the right, the massing of an excited crowd, the rising shouts, told where the trouble was.

Death to the American. Some other poor devil had been unmasked.

For a moment I thought of Susanne and Treva and that old man on the quarterdeck who had allowed me ashore. It was folly to take notice. I had my own business to think of. I was not even an American tonight. I was Lieutenant Fernández y Montoya. The thing to do was to ride on.

The cries had a wild, hysterical threat. "¡*Muerte*! ¡*Muerte*!"

I spurred into the mob, using the flat of my

saber, shouting in Mexican-Spanish: "Enough of that! Fools! An officer commands you! Stand back!"

But in that moment, nearby, flame blossomed in a fountain of death at the edge of a roof top, a shell exploded, scattering bits of the building through the night, and the mob scattered for safety.

A swaying man lurched from the front of the building where he had been cornered. I leaned from the saddle and caught his shoulder.

"Get up here, fellow! Quick!"

I doubt if he understood much. He was bleeding, groggy. It took both my hands, all my strength, to drag him up.

Then, before I could escape with him, a dozen or so horsemen wheeled into the street, questions were shouted, and answered by members of the mob, and we were surrounded.

"What is this? Where is the American?" an angry officer demanded in Spanish.

"I, Lieutenant Fernández y Montoya, have him, my Captain."

"Alive?"

"Yes, my Captain."

"Good," he said, riding across and peering. "Bring him. There will be questions. You will explain what has happened." He swore. "A cursed American inside the city, dressed as a soldier of Mexico. A spy!"

Horsemen surrounded us. There was not a chance of breaking away.

"Who the devil are you?" I muttered in his ear as we moved with the armed escort. And then, looking more closely at the cheek turned toward me, at the dark line of a scar, I knew—David Key.

The blasted idiot! I dared not even try to question him with Mexican ears so near.

David began to recover. "Cass?"

"Keep quiet, you fool," I whispered.

We rode across the great plaza, past the cathedral and the town hall. From pillar to pillar, doorway to doorway, mouth to mouth, flew word that an American spy had been captured.

I marshaled my wits. This might be bluffed through. There might be a chance, if Key would keep his mouth shut. But he hated me so, that he might grasp the chance to denounce me, even at the risk of his own neck.

We went directly to garrison headquarters. Key was marched ahead into the gloomy stone building.

The mustachioed captain strutted beside me. "A brave deed for Mexico, Lieutenant. You are wounded. How did it happen?"

"In the fighting near the Medellin road, my Captain."

"¡*Viva Méjico*!"

The big stone room we entered was bright

with candlelight and oil lamps. Officers were everywhere. Two of the troopers gripped David's arms. There was much saluting, in which I joined. Captain González, who had brought us in, began to report to a colonel.

David, too, was dressed in a lieutenant's uniform. His left sleeve was bloody. He limped, and he was bruised from the mob's beating. But now, when all was lost, he stood stiffly, coldly defiant.

Suddenly it did not matter what David did. Ice seemed to press along my spine. I turned my back to the broad-chested, thick-necked man who strolled past the door guard as if well known here at garrison headquarters. But every nerve in my body was straining for Jan Spreck's first comment.

"Well, Colonel, I hear you have an American spy," Spreck said jovially. "Dot iss good, eh?"

He strolled in front of us, and I turned away.

Then his heavy voice said: "I've seen dot scar before." He repeated it in Spanish, to David. "New Orleans, eh, Captain? You remember?"

"I have nothing to say to you, sir," David answered coldly in English.

Spreck chuckled. "Colonel," he said in Spanish, "who is the lieutenant with the bandaged head? Have I seen him before? Ah, Lieutenant . . ."

There was nothing to do but turn. All eyes were on me. Spreck's smile had such greasy satisfaction that I knew he'd recognized me the moment he entered the room.

"The stage station at Jalapa?" he pretended to recall. "Was it not there, Lieutenant? Your name is . . . ?"

The colonel, with a wave of his hand, said: "Lieutenant Fernández y Montoya is reported to have captured the spy, *señor.*"

"Good." Spreck chuckled. "You will allow me to speak with him, Colonel, while you are busy."

The colonel's hand waved assent. Jan Spreck evidently was a man of some importance among the military in Mexico.

He took my arm and walked me to the corner of the big stone-walled room. "Well, *señor,*" he said in his clumsy Spanish, "a pleasure, no?"

"Out with it. What's on your mind?"

Spreck was perspiring as he looked at me with his ponderous, fatherly air. "You know what iss waiting, my boy," he said under his breath in English. "A wall and a firing squad. Dot iss bad. But I am your friend, no?"

"Are you?"

"You will see." Spreck paused, smiling. "After you have proved we are friends. . . . You are in the city to find Miss Dexter, eh? Where is she? Speak up, my young friend. Remember what happens to a spy."

"So she got away from you," I said softly. "You're looking for her." Now I was smiling.

"Tell me where to find her, where you were to meet her, and I giff you the word of Jan Spreck you will go free and safe. Miss Dexter will not be harmed." He waited, watching my face. "Tell me."

"Then what will you do?"

"I will wait here with you." Spreck laughed softly. "*Und* when soldiers have brought Miss Dexter here, you will go. Fair enough, no?"

He had me fair, like a cat with a doomed mouse. Until he had Treva, he had me and meant to keep me.

"I don't know where Miss Dexter is," I told him truthfully.

Spreck shrugged. "Lies will not help. You would not be in Veracruz unless you knew where to look."

"If I'm put in front of a firing squad, I still won't be able to tell you where she is."

I measured the distance to the door and figured the chance of making a run for it. Spreck guessed my thought. "I haf pistols," he said. "You will be killed in trying to escape."

He was right, of course. The mob that had trailed us here to garrison quarters was still outside, beyond the guards. An escaping American spy would be torn apart.

"Have you Commodore Dexter's pass? I asked.

Spreck nodded. "It now iss not much use. But one never knows. It has helped."

"You'll trade it for Miss Dexter?"

"Only for your life will you find her," Spreck told me. His smile broadened. "Why be foolish? Life iss good, eh?" He glanced at a thick repeating watch. "Thirty seconds I will give you. Quick. Will you live for the years ahead?"

"You'll have to go with me to find her," I said. "Just you and me alone. That's final."

Spreck put the watch back. Red flowed into his perspiring face. "Young man, I stopped being a fool before you were born. We waste words, eh?" He drew a pistol from under his coat, crying: "Colonel Pedraza . . . !"

I smashed the rest of it back in his mouth with my fist and caught at his pistol as he reeled back. The weapon roared harmlessly against the edge of my hip. I tore it from his hand.

He was gabbling incoherently through a crushed mouth and broken teeth as I smashed him between the eyes with the pistol barrel.

In Spanish I shouted: "Liar! Thief! Spy! Traitor!" I drew my saber as Spreck's big body crumpled on the stone floor. "A Fernández y Montoya has been insulted by bribery!" I cried through the confusion. "Arrest this traitor!"

Shouting, waving the saber so wildly men ducked away, I rushed at Colonel Pedraza. "My Colonel! You have been betrayed! Arrest the man! Shoot him!"

By now the room was in an uproar. No one knew what to do or where to turn.

"Quiet!" Colonel Pedraza snapped at me. He started toward Spreck's sprawled figure, where other officers were already gathering.

I caught one of the troopers who held David's arm. "Quick! Assist the colonel!"

A shove and the flat of my sword sent him stumbling toward the end of the room. I did the same with the other trooper. Neither dared to dispute the command of an officer.

"Outside, if you want to try for it," I told David under my breath. I dashed for the doorway, waving saber and pistol, shouting to the guard to assist the colonel.

The door guard stumbled inside with the push I gave him. David had followed me. His face had a cold desperation.

I ran, shouting and flourishing the sword, calling help for the colonel. The rest of Captain González's troopers rushed inside, carrying the outer guard with them. The mob pressed after them, knowing no more than the troopers.

"This way," I told David.

We slipped behind the stone pillars of the portico entrance, came out into the open, and ran through the night. Jan Spreck alone could have straightened out the confusion, and Spreck was unconscious. The Mexican uniforms David and I wore were our safety for the time being.

I thrust my head bandage inside the uniform and doubled around a corner into the great plaza. A note of order seemed to be entering the uproar we had left.

"They'll be after us," I said. "Across the plaza. Keep close to me. It'll be a firing squad next time, in short order."

X

The bombardment was rising in intensity. The city guns and San Juan de Ulúa fortress off the harbor mole were replying in a frenzy. The night shook. The very pavement stones of the plaza seemed to tremble. The glare of explosions flickered and danced across the sky.

"When the siege mortars are in battery, they'll gut the city," David observed darkly. "Scott came prepared to blast it into rubble if necessary."

"He's doing well enough now," I said. "What the devil brought you in here tonight?"

"Treva brought me," David replied sulkily. "I won't have you doing more for her than I do."

"You left your duty for that?"

"No. I was sent to the front lines to observe. If I chose to enter the city, I could."

"You made a pretty stew of my plans. If it weren't for you, I'd be roaming Veracruz at my pleasure. And finding Treva and helping her. You had seven years to do for Treva and didn't marry her. Why not keep out of the way now?"

"She loves me. I love her. If it weren't for you, we'd have been married long ago." He went on angrily: "Treva was too young and romantic. You turned her head. She couldn't forget something that never existed. She'll know better now."

"Will she?" I said. "We'll see." And in that moment when David confirmed all I'd suspected about Treva's feeling for me, I thought of Susanne with a little wrench. Susanne, who had promised to bring Treva to me. Of course, Susanne could not understand; Susanne had not known Treva, or how memories could grow more tender with passing years.

"Since I'm in your way, I'll leave you," David said stiffly.

"Don't be a fool again." I caught his arm as he turned away. "We'll have to stand or fall together. Our necks will be safer. Besides, Treva might need help from you. You have that much feeling for her, haven't you, no matter what she decides? Stop hating me."

"How can I hate you after you saved my life twice?" David retorted irritably. "I just don't like you."

"Fair enough. I believe they're after us now. . . . Into the cathedral. They may not think to look for American spies in the shadow of the altar."

We joined men and women and children

214

entering the cavernous depths of the cathedral. Inside, war was muted and far away. It was quiet, save for the low drone of whispering prayers from kneeling scores. Candles burned before the great, impressive altar. Priests in gorgeous vestments were kneeling, reciting prayers. The odor of incense was sweet and heavy over the bowed heads.

"Prayer would not be amiss, even for us," I whispered to David as we went silently into the shadows at one side and knelt awkwardly.

I had not said many prayers since I had left my mother to be a midshipman. When I bowed my head now, my mother seemed very near and war seemed very far away, and the help I needed for Treva very certain there on the altar. I did not forget Susanne.

A long time later, when I lifted my head, a strange new peace was with me. I felt amazingly calm even when soldiers passed near, scanning the worshipers, although I knew they were looking for us. Presently they went away.

The peace stayed with me as I stood up. David moved with me, gloomily silent. I think he felt that this night he was losing Treva forever. He paused in tense silence when a small, wrinkled old priest in sandals and belted robe stepped up and greeted us: "God be with you, my sons."

"As God wills it, Father," I replied.

"You are fighting for your country?"

"Yes, Father."

"God suffers with all this killing," he said sadly.

"Yes, Father." A thought struck me. "Father," I said, "I look for a young lady. She must have prayed here. She is a dancer. *Señorita* Valverde."

"A friend of yours, my son?"

"Yes."

"You have prayed to find her?"

"Yes," I said truthfully.

He sighed and crossed himself. His knees bent to the altar. His wrinkled hand went to the cross hanging from his neck. "Come with me."

We followed his sandaled steps out into the night, into the tumult and the red flicker of war. I became aware that people in the plaza were being stopped and questioned. The city evidently was being searched for us. We were turning out of the plaza when a squad of soldiers came by.

"The blessings of God this night," our little old priest called to them.

Several answered respectfully as he made the sign of the cross toward them. David brushed against me. He was stiff with tension. And I, each moment, expected the outcry of discovery.

But we passed in safety with our robed guide. We followed him through darker streets and confusion. He did not look aside when a shell burst near us. He was placid as he stopped at the doorway of a house without lights, and knocked.

216

He knocked several times before an answer came through the porter's little wicket. "Yes?" a voice said—Susanne's voice.

"It is Father Gomez, from the cathedral, daughter. I have friends who seek you."

"What friends?"

"You will remember me from that last night in Havana," I said, and I heard her catch her breath inside the gate. She unbarred it. I stepped inside, and she caught my hand tightly.

Father Gomez said placidly: "I will stand here in the street and say my beads before returning. A priest might be needed by some who pass."

Susanne guided us into a candle-lit room. Her face was shining. "You did come, Cass. Nothing has happened to you." Her eyes widened. "Captain Key!"

David bowed. "Fortune of war, ma'am."

"And love," I reminded him. David flushed as I said to Susanne: "We've had a brush with Jan Spreck tonight. He's looking for Treva Dexter. You have her?"

"That pig Spreck!" Susanne said with a curl of her lip. "He has questioned me about her." She was pale as she looked at me. I knew she was thinking of that last night in Havana, and of the moment when she would see Treva and me together. I pressed her hand, overcome by such emotion as I had never before known. Things I had never till that moment dreamed of saying rose unbidden to my lips. But Susanne, oblivious, cut me short.

"I kept my promise, Cass," she said, and walked across the room and opened a door. "Treva! He is here!"

Treva was pale, too, as she came into the room. The clear candlelight struck gold glints from her chestnut hair.

"Cass!" she cried, and started to me with her hands out in welcome, as she had often met me of old.

Then she saw David Key, and stopped. "David!" she said chokingly, and went to him blindly. I doubt if they knew Susanne and I were there, as they clung together.

I had a queer, detached feeling, and—heaven help me—a sensation of relief. All my fine memories of Treva through the years seemed to be dissolving in a desire to show these two how a lover should greet a loved one—how a girl such as Susanne would respond to such a meeting. David was holding Treva so damned properly, and she, God help her, seemed to think it the height of happiness.

They were both pink and glowing when they turned to us, and, I did no more then than to take Susanne's hand again in mine.

"Thank God," David said huskily. He gave me a tolerant and triumphant look.

"We'll still have to help a little," I said dryly.

"We're still in Veracruz. If we're not rooted out and shot as spies, we'll have the town shelled down about us." I turned to Susanne. Sadness and pity were in the look she gave me. "Will you leave tonight also?" I asked her. "When the siege lines are drawn and the full bombardment starts, it will be too late."

"Whatever you think, Cass."

"Then get cloaks. Shawls, too, if you have them. Are you agreed, Captain?"

"Naturally," David assented.

"I'll ask the priest if he can guide Treva and Susanne ahead of us. If you and I are caught, Father Gomez can bring them back here."

In the darkness outside the gate Father Gomez listened attentively.

"All women should leave Veracruz," he agreed. "I will walk with the *señoritas* to the city gate."

Before we started, there was time for a hurried explanation as to how Susanne had located Treva.

In Mexico City, Susanne had found Spreck and had his movements watched. He often went to a rented villa outside the city, and servants had revealed that a young American lady was held prisoner there. The rest was careful planning, liberal bribes, and, finally, a dangerous coach ride to Veracruz.

Susanne had not believed that Spreck would come so quickly to Veracruz, looking for Treva. But he had, and his powerful links with the military, and the uses to which Treva might be put as a prisoner, had made dangerous any attempt to get her out of the city, even to escape the American bombardment.

"I think you did not come too soon, Cass," Susanne told me. She was not happy that I had lost Treva. The sadness was still in each look she gave me. I knew she was thinking of how I must be hurt. She could think that way because she was Susanne. Her faint smile could not hide the stiffness of her lips. "I shall be glad to go, Cass. I think to Spain, next. They like me in Madrid."

"At the moment," I said, "you're going to the city gate. That's far enough ahead to plan."

The girls were ready to leave. They wore thin dark cloaks and long fringed shawls over their heads. In the Veracruz night they would be old crones, for all a stranger could tell.

Father Gomez was inside the gate. He was troubled. "I have been asked if strangers have entered this house," he told us. He crossed himself. "I gave God's blessing and said I was not the watchman in the night."

"Who asked, Father?"

"A big man who did not speak the language of the country well."

"Jan Spreck!" I muttered. "Where is this man, Father?"

"He went toward the plaza."

"Take the young ladies the other way," I

decided. "First, I'll step outside. He may be waiting with help."

"He'll kill you, Cass."

"Do as I say, Susanne."

She looked at me long, then drew the black shawl across her face.

I stepped out into the dark street, saber drawn. I saw no one there and motioned to Father Gomez that it was safe to lead Treva and Susanne away.

The city was shaking under exploding shells. The deep thunder of heavy cannon was like a restless storm, which wheeled above one spot, never moving on. People ran past us in the street.

"I think we can follow now," I said to David, and we hurried until we were behind Father Gomez and the two girls.

The old priest led us through the city by dark and roundabout streets, walking calmly through shell fire and growing desolation.

The great gate by which I had entered the city was the last test. It might be closed. Guards might be posted there, watching for David and me.

We did find guards at the gate, and confusion, and very little light. As we neared it, Father Gomez began to intone a litany. A woman carrying a heavy bundle fell in with Treva and Susanne, and called the responses, in a shrill and quavering voice. Others joined in, both men and women.

"Close up with them," I said to David, and we

became part of a growing procession that moved through the night, praising God.

The guards at the gate did not stop or search that procession of prayer and faith. We passed safely outside, and there David and I joined Treva and Susanne. Father Gomez ended his litany and gave blessing to those who went on to safety. Then he turned to us.

"My children, go in peace," he said. "You will reach the Americans now in safety, I think."

"You knew?" I asked, startled.

Quietly, he said: "There could be only two men, one with a scar on his face, who the soldiers were seeking in the cathedral."

"Knowing that, you helped us? You, a Mexican, with our guns firing on you?"

I heard him sigh. I saw his hand go to the big cross hanging at his belt. "Prayer shall be answered," he said quietly. "You prayed to God, and could God do less than answer? Go now with God. Pray for those who stay."

He left us, a meek and gentle old man, trudging back into the city, which shortly would be sealed against escape.

Susanne took my hand and looked after him. "With God," I heard her repeat. And then the four of us went on, hurrying against the coming of dawn.

The skirmishing parties and the outposts of the Mexican forces were not watching for Americans to appear from the direction of the city walls. We were stopped again and again, but David's and my uniforms kept us safe.

Dawn was bringing the palest of gray over the eastern sky when we climbed a sand hill and rested on the top.

"The stone magazine should be near here," I said. "We'd best wait for more light. American sentries might shoot."

David moved to Treva. They sat down, decently apart, and talked in low tones. Susanne and I stood there, watching dawn creep from the Mexican Gulf, behind the tall masts of the fleet.

I put my arm around Susanne. There was just enough light to see how tired and sad she looked.

"I'm sorry, Cass," she said.

"Sorry?"

"Of course. That it was not you. I . . . I didn't even know, myself, until she saw him. I would not have you hurt, Cass."

There was much to say, and suddenly I was awkward about how to say it. The light was growing brighter. The thunder of the guns had slacked off.

"I must go back to the fleet," I said. "I don't know what will happen to me. But if you are somewhere, thinking about me, Susanne, it will be easier."

Her fingers tightened on my hand. "I shall pray for you, Cass."

"Prayer shall be answered," I quoted Father Gomez. I had to fumble for words, because of what I felt. "Susanne, in the cathedral, on my knees, I prayed for you. That you would be happy and safe. That you would have love and faith without ending."

"Then I shall, Cass, if you asked it," she said tightly. "Wherever I am."

"Where you are, I'll be too, if you'll have it," I said. "There never could have been anyone but you, Susanne. Do you believe me?"

The dawn was on Susanne's face as she looked up at me, and an inner glow through her weariness had more beauty than any dawn could ever bring.

"I am afraid to believe you, Cass." She turned, and her arms went around me. "But, Cass, my dear, hold me close, Cass."

So I held her close, the sweetness of her against me and all about me, and I whispered: "*Querida mia* . . . my beloved, *te amo* . . . I love you. . . ."

HUNTED WOLF

I

At the empty rock seep called Phantom Pool, Tom Buckner waited to gamble his last cartridge against a mangy wolf that one of them would eat the other and reach the sweet waters in the Mustang Hills alive for the next kill. Buckner's swollen lips twisted at the thought. Living to kill Hal Stafford had become a frantic urge since Buckner had plodded out of the shimmering distance and found Phantom Pool dry and realized why Stafford and his riders had turned back.

Stafford had known Buckner's wounded horse wouldn't last. Stafford must have known the pool was dry. He'd probably laughed, big head thrown back, eyes closing a little, mirth shaking his deep chest. Stafford's humor could appreciate Buckner's walking deeper into dry country, to the dry basin of Phantom Pool. Why press hard and dangerous pursuit to kill a man when the desert would do it with slow and exquisite agony?

They hadn't known Buckner was down to his last cartridge; they'd known well enough what his gun could do. After his horse had gone down, Buckner had slogged on afoot, saving the last cartridge for a last try at Stafford. Two hours back, when he rounded the point of sun-baked red rock and sighted heat-cracked mud in the bottom of Phantom Pool basin, he'd known why Stafford had turned back.

The wolf had a gaunt, starved, dried-out look, too. It was an old-man wolf, tough and stringy, and certainly wise with the years. And thirsty now, like Buckner was thirsty—god-awful, agonizingly, hopelessly thirsty.

The wolf had come along the rock slope, through the late afternoon's shimmering heat, man-scent uncaught until the critter topped the hot, jumbled rocks just above the dry basin. Not a hundred feet away, Buckner eyed the wolf. Food stood there—food tough and stringy—but food. And moisture, red and life-giving. The wolf was thinking the same thing, thinking like a wolf. And Tom Buckner was thinking like a wolf, too.

The thought caught at Buckner. The wolf would never think like a man. But Buckner had been thrown straight back to a wolf. Kill or be killed; eat or be eaten. It took hold, deep, primitive, and savage, while swollen tongue stirred and breath stepped up. The wolf faded back among the hot rocks, limping but agile, and Buckner felt furious regret that he'd hesitated. He forced himself to remain calm. Only death waited out in the desert, even for the wolf. It had that dried-out, end-of-trail look. Here they were at Phantom Pool; here they'd stay until one ate the other.

Buckner managed a wry grin. He was thinking

like the wolf. He could outwait the wolf and reach the hills and cool water, and see Susan Todd, if only for an hour, on his way to find Stafford. He put away the thought of Susan Todd, as he had many times since yesterday. There lay weakness and regret.

The hot rocks lifted straight up a full thirty feet at the back and north side of the pool basin. On the south side the boulder-covered slope came down steeply. The west rim of the dry basin was open. Some forty yards out, an eroded outcropping of red rock offered scant shade against the brazen sun now drifting lower. Tom Buckner sat at the base of the outcropping, waiting.

The wolf returned on the rock above the basin, thirty feet up. The tip of his nose barely showed beside a wind-scoured boulder. Tom Buckner, hunched immobile, arms locked around his knees, gazed fixedly on that scant bit of grizzled wolf muzzle. Susan Todd came into his thoughts again, a smiling, quiet girl, with thoughtful eyes and enduring sweetness, no matter what her mood. A man felt more a man when with Susan. At least Buckner had felt that way often and had guessed other men must also. Not because Susan was strong, or any weakness of Susan's played up to a man. And there lay a puzzle Buckner had wanted to solve and would yet solve, he promised himself.

The grizzled muzzle and close-laid ears were

visible. Each time Buckner moved even slightly, the wolf shrank back and vanished. Buckner damned the animal, croaking the words painfully in his rough, dry throat. The wolf's right ear pricked. The eyes watched steadily. Buckner whipped out the gun. The wolf vanished. Buckner had known he would. That muzzle was not a target for the last cartridge anyway. It had to be a close and certain shot.

Shortly the wolf was watching again. He was an old wise lobo who could wait. Who meant to wait. Buckner put away all anger, which was weakness. He had to out-wolf the wolf, be calmer, more patient, stronger. He must do it to live.

Stronger than a wolf. Buckner was amused once more. He had hunted wolves. Shot them. Trapped them. Always his guns and traps had made him the stronger. Now the wolf and he were equal across the heat-cracked mud of the dry basin. Now was he stronger with patience to wait and wait?

The wolf could wait without irritation, without anger or nervousness. It was the heat, probably, and the thirst—the God-awful nagging thirst—which made Buckner consider the wolf an equal, who had his own thirst and problem of waiting. A man could feel sorry for the wolf. For when the showdown came, the wolf would have no gun. He could be all that Tom Buckner was, in will, in patience, and in caution. As good as Tom Buckner. But he had no gun. There was a problem about it, like the puzzle of Susan Todd. The wolf, meeting heat and thirst and power of will, was as good as Tom Buckner—but he had no gun.

Brief twilight flung crimson across the high sky. The wolf had not moved when solid night closed in. Moonrise was more than an hour off. Buckner waited. If he hunted the wolf, it would fade away before him. But if the wolf hunted Buckner, it would come close, in the open. The one cartridge was enough. But the wolf was unarmed. Buckner pondered the thought—no gun.

He guessed the wolf would move before moonrise. A bit of breeze finally wandered past. The night had a great empty weight of silence. Then Buckner held his breath. Soft, rhythmic sounds, barely audible, were somewhere in front of him. Slowly Buckner brought the gun muzzle up across one cramped knee. The sounds continued. They were puzzling; they had no meaning, until Buckner finally sorted out the truth. Rock at the back and side of the pool basin formed a sounding board. The wolf was digging in the cracked mud at the back of the basin. Digging before moonrise, in frantic haste, while movements were hidden. The wolf hadn't been able to wait.

Buckner came up noiselessly, stiff, aching. He almost staggered with the first cautious forward step, gun cocked and ready. The wolf's labor evidently masked the fainter slither of Buckner's advance. Once more Buckner wanted to chortle. The wolf hadn't been able to wait. Then a sudden scurry of limping flight whisked close in the dim starlight. For an instant the wolf was a passing shadow, his gasping audible as he broke for safety. The Colt's muzzle lined clearly on the target.

Tom Buckner stood there on the cracked mud and cursed thickly. He'd remembered the wolf had no gun and had held the shot. Crazy from thirst, evidently. Tom Buckner licked dry lips with dry tongue and tried to think it out. Finally, he went forward and held a lighted match where the wolf had been digging.

The rock wall bent in a little at the bottom. The mud there was just as dry, heat cracks as deep. But almost against the rock, the wolf had been clawing down in an inch-wide mud crack. The hole was dry. Buckner swore in futile helplessness. Then his queer respect for the wolf came at him. The wolf had a reason for digging there.

Decades of passing men had left trash of forgotten camps around Phantom Pool. Old cans, bottles, char of campfires, and litter, how deep no man knew. There were bones too, in plenty. Buckner recalled a wheel hub with several spokes, out about a hundred yards. He walked out to it, forcing himself to move deliberately. Haste could spark false hope and flare into the frantic end.

He wrenched out a loose wagon wheel spoke and whittled the dry wood to a point. He found a stout tin can and had his pick and shovel. He dug in the wolf's hole until he was breathing harshly, like the wolf had been breathing. Two feet down it did seem a little damper. But only damp. Three feet down Buckner threw another can of dirt and lay on his belly, panting weakly. His arm hung down in the hole as he lay full length, not caring much anymore. When strength drained out of a man, hope could drain out too.

The cool wet seep was on his fingers before he realized what was happening. He snatched the fingers to his mouth. *Wet.* And wet when he did it again. He scraped an ounce of muddy water in the can, and sucked the wetness deep in his mouth, and held it, and let it crawl sandy and wet down his dry throat. And still the water seeped into the hole. The wolf had been right. Later, quite sane and growing stronger, Buckner carried the can full of water out into the desert and sat down. The moon had bloomed full and bright. Buckner watched the wolf approach the hole. Only Buckner himself could know how the wolf felt about that muddy seep of life.

Presently the wolf headed, limping, toward the far hills. Buckner watched with the ghost of an understanding smile. And in turn, carrying a quart whiskey bottle of water in each hand, he also started for the hills. The look on Hal Stafford's face would be worth all this. And there was also the matter of Susan Todd, if only for an hour. That puzzle about Susan.

II

The next blistering afternoon Buckner was in Black Cañon. Meacham's Keg, ahead of him, was the first water where a man was not apt to be sighted and reported. His feet were raw and swollen. The water bottles were long empty and discarded. Buckner was dried-out, weary, limping, but not staggering. He'd slept a little before and after dawn. A hard and fit man could go for a week without food. It was water he must have.

A sloughing whisper of sound came drifting through the cañon silence. Buckner halted and listened intently. He might have scrambled up the rock-piled bench slope at his right. Instead he ran forward a dozen yards and crouched behind a great water-smoothed boulder. He cocked the handgun with its single cartridge.

A horse came cantering slowly on the flood-scoured cañon bed. One horse, as Buckner had gambled. It was almost to the rock when he stood up. The startled dun horse snorted and half whirled away. Young Curly Powers, a Stafford rider, swore loudly, reined the horse hard, and reached fast for his revolver.

"Don't try it, Curly!"

Powers decided not to, and lifted high his gun hand as he quieted the horse. All Stafford's men knew Buckner's skill with a gun.

"Step down on this side, Curly. Keep that hand up. Unbuckle that belt and let it drop."

Curly Powers probably would have gambled against one shot. But he didn't know there was only one. Disarmed, he stood in sullen apprehension, blond and young, and dangerous, too, because he was jumpy.

"Walk back up the cañon, Curly."

"Going to shoot me in the back?"

"Might. You were with the bunch trying to target my back. Get going."

Curly moved slowly. Buckner buckled on the gun belt with its welcome glint of shiny brass cartridges filling each loop. He reloaded his own gun and tossed Curly's emptied gun on the sand. Only when he checked the saddle carbine and found it ready for use did he drink sparingly from the saddle canteen.

Then in the saddle he relaxed for one glorious moment, aches, weariness, hunger of small matter now. Curly halted with sullen tenseness when Buckner rode up beside him and asked: "Who's riding out this way with you?"

"No one." The lie was cloudy and angry in Curly's pale eyes.

Buckner contemplated him. "Curly, working for Stafford won't do you any good. You're young enough to slope on and do better."

"Never mind how young I am. You hired out to Stafford."

"And quit." Buckner's throat still felt gravelly, but an impulse made him speak on. "Stafford gave me an idea his bunch was being hazed around by other outfits. He's convincing when he talks to a stranger. When I saw it was Stafford doing the pushing, I quit."

"Trying to preach to me?"

"Sort of," Buckner said. He could look back a few years, and he'd been hot-headed too, like Curly. Sure of himself. Not wanting advice. "You saw what happened to me, Curly. I quit. Took a room at the hotel in Luna. Minding my own business before I moved on. But I'd seen too much to suit Stafford, I guess. His men came crowding me into a fight. That way, Stafford had me, he thought, being he was a deputy on the side, and able to take his men after me . . . same thing might happen to you."

"Not me," Curly denied. His lip thrust out in swaggering confidence. "When I quit fat pay like Stafford's, I won't be fool enough to camp close to the girl Stafford's running after."

"That's fool talk."

"Tell Stafford," said Curly. "Me, I'm only after wages and extra money I can pick up. Stafford's got it. It's forty miles to the ranch from here. You going to leave me on foot?"

Buckner's own look was cloudy over the thing Curly had suggested. "Your gun is back there on the sand. Next time don't come heading off a man who might be walking back dry from Phantom Rocks. Walk home or stay at Meacham's water until they send for you." Buckner shook the dun horse into a lope up the cañon.

He should have known Curly better—young, hot-tempered. The surprise shot Curly fired after him gouged violently along Buckner's side. The left side. He lurched to the right. That, and a hard rein wheeling the horse, made Curly's second shot miss. The echoes boomed off the cañon walls as the horse came around. Buckner's gun was in his hand. Anger had him in a misty wave. He saw the small, double-barreled derringer in Curly's hand. Not much range to that tiny gun, but the heavy slugs were deadly at close quarters. Curly was scrambling to the shelter of another boulder. He made it inches ahead of the shot Buckner fired.

Buckner halted the horse. Gun cocked, he watched the boulder. The rage began to drain out of him. "Should have listened to me, Curly!" he called.

Curly's reply was sullen again behind the

boulder. "It was worth a try for the five hundred Stafford offered if you were sighted."

"And killed?"

"You ain't any good to Stafford alive."

The wounded left side was bleeding. Buckner noted the bullet had passed out through his shirt front. It could be worse.

"You haven't got a chance!" he told Curly.

"Who said I had?"

"Don't ever get near me again! I'll kill you on sight!"

Buckner wheeled the dun horse fast up the cañon. Curly had been a dead one and knew it. But killing Curly wouldn't solve anything. He was useless as a prisoner. Stafford was the business ahead.

A man named Meacham had sunk a keg at the foot of a towering sandstone cliff where Indian well water seeped out and vanished in the scoured sand of the cañon bed. The old keg held water, crystal and sweet. Buckner knew of it by hearsay. He found the keg—and fresh sign of shod horses by it. Two horses.

Curly Powers had come this way with a companion. They had watered and split up. But the other man might have been near enough to hear the shots. He might be riding back now, or already set in ambush, to earn Stafford's five hundred. Buckner drank, refilled the canteen, then looked to his side. He had made a pad of his

238

neckerchief and held it over the wound. Bleeding had almost stopped. A rib was chipped or broken. There was pain.

The afternoon was drawing on. It was only a matter of time before Curly joined the other horseman. One of them would either try to follow him, or get word fast to Hal Stafford.

Buckner was desperately weary as he started the long ride to Luna. Stafford was often in town at night. He would be this night, Buckner felt certain. With some of his men, as usual. Buckner discounted the men. This was not a fight. It was an execution. Stafford was always armed and ready for trouble. This time he would have it. The wolf-like urge to get at Stafford had not abated. It was the same chill certainty that had held Buckner steady at Phantom Pool. He could out-wolf the wolf. He would out-wolf Stafford. This time there would be more than one cartridge. And one more thing. One thing all Stafford's craftiness could not judge. Buckner didn't care what happened to himself. It was a wolf-like savageness new to Stafford's experience.

Buckner returned to the puzzle of Susan Todd. Stafford had been more than friendly with Susan. If she was aware of the man's bullying, out-reaching ways, she'd never said. The dun horse pricked ears as Buckner said aloud: "That fool Curly."

Then Buckner thought how he'd stayed on in

Luna after quitting Stafford. Usually he'd have ridden on toward new country. Luna wasn't a town to hold a man. He'd told himself he'd wanted a rest. Now he pondered that Luna stay. The town and Susan Todd kept running together in his thoughts. There was a problem there, like the wolf that had no gun, but Buckner was too tired now for problems. He had the one last thing to do. Get Stafford. Nothing else mattered much.

The afternoon tailed out as he threaded badlands east of the Mustang Hills. He kept to the low washes and draws, below the ridges, hidden from prying eyes on some distant rise. The canteen emptied too quickly. More water meant at least a ten-mile jog off the direct line to Luna. Buckner rode dry and was thankful when night took the land under bright stars.

Luna was eighty-odd miles from the railroad. There was a daily through stage. Another stage line ran from Luna across the mountains, tapping cow and mining settlements to the northeast. The adobe and board sprawl of the town lay on Luna Creek Flats, beside the first sharp rise of the mountain foothills. Not a county seat. Deputy law was all the town had. A man could jump across the clear, chuckling shallows of Luna Creek. But the cold brawling current and underground water were enough for the town, enough for trees, bushes, and a few little irrigated gardens.

The town lights were bright points against the darker foothills as Buckner rode in. Rider and horse were both dead beat. A small night breeze sliding off the foothills tainted the darkness pleasantly with town scent of wood smoke. The aching fatigue lifted a bit. Buckner's purpose began to tighten nerves and pull energy from the deep core of his hard frame. The horse, too, stepped more lightly.

They passed the half-hearted barking of the first dogs, the scatter of outlying shacks, and swung toward the compound at the rear of the Luna House. Buckner was gambling that warning of his return had not yet reached town. Several horses fed in the open-front shed at the back of the compound. No lantern, no loiterers near the spot. Buckner watered the horse at the pump trough, unsaddled, and left the animal at a waiting manger in the feed shed. Only then, carrying Curly's carbine, did he walk stiffly to the back of the hotel, pain feverish in his side.

The clapboard hotel was two stories high, with a railed gallery at the front facing the street and shed-roofed porch at the back. The back windows upstairs were dark. Kitchen windows showed light. Kitchen door was closed. So was a second door giving into the back of the passage which ended in the lobby. When Buckner opened that hall door, murmur of talk in the lobby drifted to him. The shadowy back stairs creaked under his quiet ascent to the upper corridor.

His room rent had been paid up. When he unlocked the door and stepped in and struck a match, everything was as he had left it. This could easily seem one more pleasant evening in the string of Luna days after leaving Stafford's hire.

Buckner pulled down the shade at the back window and lighted the glass lamp. He carried the lamp to the washstand mirror and eyed his reflection. Dirty, unshaven, gaunt. Smiling ruefully, Buckner got out his razor and stripped off his shirt.

Shaving and washing helped. But the face was still gaunt, eyes bloodshot, fatigue etched deeply. His middle curved in, hard and empty. The wound was a raw furrow over a rib, which was probably cracked. Halves of a clean towel knotted together made a fair bandage. He was pulling on a clean shirt when heavy steps tramped off the front stairs into the corridor. Buckner blew out the lamp and listened to the steps pause, a door being unlocked.

He heard the clear tones of Susan Todd's voice and stood motionless, shirt half buttoned. Susan's father, a sickly man who seldom left his room, owned the hotel. Susan ran the place firmly, competently. The door closed. Susan's lighter steps came on back in the hall and stopped before

Buckner's door. Susan stood there a moment. Darkness clotted about Buckner. Susan could not suspect anyone was in the room. But her key scraped in the lock.

Buckner had locked the door and left the key there. Now the push of Susan's key on the outside backed Buckner's key out of the lock. It clinked audibly on the floor. Susan stood quietly for another long moment. Then her key opened the lock and she pushed the door open.

"Come out!" Susan ordered sharply.

The yellow flare of a match blossomed against Buckner's thumbnail.

"I'll light the lamp," he said, and it came to him this was the hour he wanted. And queerly, because it was the last hour before he sought Stafford, he met it with reluctance.

He heard Susan catch breath audibly. She stepped in, closed the door. The whiter lamp glow flooded the room and Tom Buckner looked at her with puckered intentness, as if this were a first meeting. Susan's warm, brown hair was piled on her head. She had smooth white skin and there was a deftness about all her movements.

She stood quite still now. Buckner could not know his bloodshot intentness put an inflexible cast to his features as Susan asked with a hint of demanding breathlessness: "Why did you come back?"

Buckner fumbled with the remaining buttons of

his shirt. Curly's gun belt hung in a heavy slant around his middle. The carbine leaned against the end of the oak washstand, with its burden of white pottery pitcher and bowl. Susan had known he was one of Stafford's fighting men. Her manner was judging him now, hired gunslinger, trouble seeker.

"I needed a shave." He touched the gaunt, sun-cured smoothness the blade had left.

Susan's hostility seemed to grow. Buckner could understand it. Stafford's best man had provoked the fight in the Eagle Bar, adjoining the hotel. The gunfire had been audible through the small town. Susan had been witness to the gathering rush of Stafford's other men, while Buckner had retreated through the back door of the Eagle, to his horse behind the hotel, and left town. He hadn't wanted more trouble. He'd ridden from Stafford's Cross-T men to think over the obviously planned pattern of the potentially deadly incident. Only when they came after him and stayed after him had he realized they were riding for a kill. Hal Stafford's men never moved without Stafford's orders.

"They said you escaped across the desert. You didn't ride back for a shave."

"I walked part of the way."

Susan hardly seemed to hear him. The shadow of some memory darkened in her look. "You shot a man. The law wants you."

"Stafford wants me. I had to kill Morrison, or let him kill me."

"Morrison is only badly wounded. If you give yourself up, it will work out."

He hunched big shoulders. The movement drew pain from his side. "Give up to Stafford?" His sarcastic smile disposed of that.

"Why did you quit the Cross T?" Susan asked abruptly.

"Didn't like the way Stafford operates. He wants everything in sight and doesn't care how he gets it. Or have you been looking the other way lately?"

Susan's ghost of a flush seemed to point up increasing hostility.

Buckner thought with etching disapproval: *She's worried about him.* He got a measure of cold satisfaction in knowing she should be worried, if that was the way she felt.

Susan glanced away from the edge of his look and saw the blood-stiff blue neckcloth on the washstand. She stepped toward it to make sure. "What happened out there? You walked back from where?" She was calm with an effort, then she was urgent.

"First man who sighted me put a lucky bullet in my horse. It kept bleeding, put me afoot about fifteen miles this side of Phantom Pool. When I walked there, the pool was dry. I'd started without water anyway. So I walked back to Black Cañon."

"All that way without water? You couldn't. No man could. I know that Phantom Pool stretch and what happens without water."

"There was a wolf," Buckner said, smiling at the memory.

He told her, and Susan listened intently, studying his face. Abruptly she asked: "Why didn't you shoot the wolf, as you planned?"

Buckner's reflective smile considered it again. "He was almost as good a man as I was, the way we were waiting for who caved first. But he didn't have a gun."

"Gun?" said Susan. She sounded unbelieving. "Even when there was no chance of water and it might get you back, you let that stop you?"

"Next chance I'd have dropped him," Buckner said sheepishly. "A dried-out man gets light-headed."

Susan nodded. "How bad are you hurt? Does it need attention?"

"Not now."

"When did you eat last?"

"I'll get around to it."

"After you kill Hal Stafford?"

"He's one wolf who has got a gun."

"You must not!"

Buckner shrugged again, not intending to argue the point.

Susan said rather desperately, half to herself: "I'll stop you. I'll warn him."

"I want him warned. He'll have his chance at me then."

"His men are in town, too. They'll kill you."

"Might not," Buckner said indifferently.

Susan saw the futility of talk and backed against the door. She turned the key quickly and pulled it out, and caught up his fallen key, and clutched both tightly. Buckner thought: *She's turning into a wildcat to help him.* In a way he admired her spirit, while it pulled him apart and condemned him.

Susan warned sharply: "The sheriff came in on the stage. He's the law in town tonight. And he's staying here."

"When will he be here in the hotel?"

"Any minute now."

Buckner smiled again at the way he'd drawn the sheriff's absence from the hotel out of her, blocking any threat that the sheriff was downstairs. He stepped to the lamp and blew it out. In the instant blackness hid them from each other, he moved past the washstand, catching up the carbine and continuing to the back window.

His soft, unhurried voice came back at her. "I'll leave while the sheriff's out. If you try an alarm, it should draw Stafford." He ran the shade up, pushed the window up, straddled the sill when his foot found the weather-warped shingles of the back porch. He looked back into the dark, silent room. "When a wolf comes at a man's back, he

247

has to be handled. And Stafford always takes the back, which is why I quit him. You might remember it if you miss him too much."

Susan's low and shaken helplessness came at him from the dark. "How can I reason with a hot-headed fool like you are tonight?"

It made him think of his advice to Curly Powers. He straddled the sill, holding to the episode with young Curly, only vaguely conscious he was using it to draw out this last moment of parting. He heard Susan moving, but a sound in the night outside intruded and drew all his alert attention.

III

The back door of the Eagle Bar, some forty yards south of the hotel, had opened. Men were emerging. The moon was up but a belt of heavy shadow lay behind the hotel and the Eagle. The men over there were all but invisible. Their talk came through the quiet night, and the back wall of the hotel gathered it clearly.

Hal Stafford's heavy-chest tones said: "We can talk out here. That bunch in there suspected something was up, the way you came in fast, Curly. So Buckner walked out of it, damn him, and got your horse and guns?"

Young Curly's quick answer was sulky. "He jumped up under my horse's nose in Black

Cañon. Had his gun almost in my ribs. Think you'd have done different, Mister Stafford?"

"I wasn't there. Did Buckner say where he was heading . . . give any hint at all?"

"No. When Chris came along and let me have his horse, I didn't try to work out Buckner's trail. He'd have been watching for it. I thought you'd want to know quick."

"Right," agreed Stafford. "Buckner back trailed to town here, of course."

Susan had reached the window as the men emerged. Her touch on Buckner's arm had been urgent. But not holding him. Her fingers stayed on his arm as if trying to tell him something by contact.

Her hand pulled away quickly when Stafford's flat, assured chest tones said: "He has a woman on his mind bad enough to come back here and see her again. If he does, we'll get him."

A third voice asked: "Why so proddy about gettin' him?"

Stafford's coldness was immediate. "When a man quits me like Buckner did, he's against me. I don't give him a chance."

Young Powers's sulkiness lifted again. "He had a good start. If he's that lovesick a fool, maybe he's already here." Sarcasm laced Curly's next words. "If we knew who the girl was, we'd know where to look for him."

"I know," Stafford said. A thickening of

249

violence was in the admission. "Buckner wouldn't be fool enough to leave his horse in the hotel shed there. But have a look, Tex. Then we'll see what's going on in the hotel."

Young Curly said: "Buckner could have killed me. Any man would in his place. But he didn't, damn him. I'm out of the rest of this."

"Losing your nerve?"

Curly said dangerously: "Don't call me yellow, Mister Stafford. I made a long try for your five hundred, with a rabbity little derringer against my Colt shooter he had. On the showdown, he didn't kill me. I've reported in. That fills my hand. Pay me off if you like."

"Later, Curly, later. If you aren't helping now, keep out of the way."

The door opening and slamming over there was Curly's going back into the Eagle Bar in a temper.

Stafford's voice primed with an ugly rasp. "Another one against us!"

Smooth tones sounded like Fred Kistler, a sandy, long-faced, mostly silent and dangerous man. "You offered five hundred for Buckner. How much is Curly worth now?"

"Not now," said Stafford impatiently.

A crumbling, waist-high adobe wall bounded the hotel yard. Tex had stepped over and walked back through moonlight to the open-front shed.

His match spurted flame . . . then another match.

Tex's fast steps thudded back to the low fence. "Buckner's horse is there!"

A rising ugliness larded Stafford's decision. "He's in the hotel with her. Tex, you and Red watch the back. We'll go in the front."

"Sheriff's in town," Fred Kistler reminded.

"He knows Buckner's wanted. I'm deputy. Made you all a posse hunting him, didn't I? Buckner's still worth five hundred. What more do you want?"

Kistler suggested: "If Curly made it a thousand . . ."

"Your back has been scratchy against Curly's cockiness," said Stafford. His shrewd trading way settled it. "Curly's fired, as of now. Do what you like. Let's cork Buckner in the hotel."

Buckner swung back into the dark room. He brushed against Susan and stepped away. Her nearness, for some reason, set his pulses pumping.

"Fool talk," he said, and tried to make it gruff.

"Yes," Susan agreed. She was close, yet her thin-spoken coolness put distance between them. A great distance. "You couldn't feel like they said and come back to kill a man."

The racing moments were life and death. But Buckner argued: "Why not? This is between

Stafford and me. You overheard his side of it. Give me the door key."

"Men!" said Susan. "Blind and stubborn. I'll tell you why not. A killing will outlaw you. If you aren't killed also, you'll have to run. You can never come back. No man would choose that if he had thought for a woman."

Their voices, instinctively, were low inside the open window. The flying seconds made lingering folly. But this was the hour he'd wanted, the last chance to settle the puzzle of Susan. His throat felt dry again, and his pulse was fast.

"A woman who's thinking about another man . . . ?"

"A woman I don't know then," said Susan.

"Why, why . . . ," said Buckner helplessly. He struggled with it. "A man who came in as a hired gunman . . . a hardcase?"

"Perhaps if you'd killed the wolf or Curly Powers," said Susan. "But the man who *didn't* kill them is the one I'm talking to."

It came to Buckner then, like clear light. The puzzle of Susan, who looked to the best in a man, had been the puzzle of himself instead. He hadn't cared what happened to Tom Buckner tonight. Now suddenly he did care. And it was too late.

Susan was moving to the door. He moved with her in the dark. "There's nothing I can do," he told her. "Stafford's coming in after me."

252

Susan was fumbling the key into the lock. "Not Hal Stafford," she said, and she sounded stifled. "He'll send men in after you."

"It works out the same."

"Nothing works out, or this wouldn't be," said Susan as the door came open. "I'm going for the sheriff."

One quick stride carried him out into the lamp-lit hall, scanning the back and front stair heads. Susan was walking fast to the front stairs.

Buckner caught up with her, taller by a head, shoulders broad and wiry, cartridge-filled gun belt snug about the starved leanness of his middle. He moved with loose-limbed lightness, carbine in left hand, right hand easy near the belt holster as they started down.

Susan had a pinched whiteness. She blinked several times. Her silence had a finality which plucked at Buckner as nothing else had. He'd preached a steadier way for Curly's hot-headed recklessness. It should have been to Tom Buckner. Should have been . . .

His arm checked Susan at the turn of the landing, while he scanned the small rather shabby lobby, holding six, eight men and idle talk through a gray-blue drift of tobacco smoke. They were cattlemen, townsmen, and two who looked like drummers.

Adam Ingalls, who raised horses south of the Cross-T range, glanced from his hide-covered chair toward the sound of descending steps. Ingalls, a big man with a full grizzled beard, looked hard, as if not believing, and stood up with quick instinct of trouble.

"Ingalls, be comfortable," Buckner said in brief warning as he came off the steps. Susan was almost at his side.

More men were on their feet. The drummers were puzzled by the abrupt shift to wire-hard tension.

Susan's clear voice demanded, "Mister Ingalls, where is the sheriff?"

Buckner weighed each man's face as he continued to the door. "No time for that, Ingalls," he said as he passed. Adam Ingalls was no friend to Stafford. Nor was any of the others, so far as Buckner knew. He had to leave them at his back anyway, while he stepped fast through the doorway and to the left in the shadows where his eyes could adjust to the light.

Tobacco smoke drifted over the verandah railing. The pale red gleam of a cigarette tip glowed. Buckner's expanding sight made out the figure standing under the verandah rail. His gun came out and cocked, and he crouched a little as three more indistinct figures cut across the yard. By guess he knew those three. They crossed a swath of moonlight: Stafford, Fred Kistler at his left, and it looked like Roney Metcalfe at Stafford's right.

The long wide verandah was cluttered with chairs. The patch of yard held two towering cottonwoods which cast deep shadow clear to the front hitch rack and moon-drenched street dust. Lights in Paddy Henderson's store across the street seemed far away.

Stafford and his men were near the steps when Susan came out with Adam Ingalls. The men halted. Susan and Ingalls saw them just as Stafford called: "Susan, where's Buckner?"

Susan's pause was the catching of a breath. Then Susan replied clearly: "His room is upstairs." She started to descend the steps.

Adam Ingalls caught her arm. "Back inside," Ingalls rumbled in his beard.

The smoker under the verandah rail spoke with a repressed jeer. "Kistler! How much am I worth now?"

All three men whirled to the sound. Kistler's voice was dangerous. "Curly! He stopped inside the Eagle door and listened."

"Sure did," Curly agreed. "Nice listening."

Adam Ingalls propelled Susan fast, back through the doorway. Ingalls swung around then, filling the doorway with his solid bulk, watching.

Hal Stafford's anger slurred with restraint. "Some other time, Curly. This is the law now."

"Hell of a law with you, Kistler, and Metcalfe for samples!" Curly's tone rode his own windy, jumpier anger. "I owe Buckner a turn. Get the sheriff to take him. I've got things to tell the sheriff anyway."

Buckner let out a sigh of decision and came full upright. Curly was riding hot-headed anger with spurs, running over them. And with little chance against all three. In odd surprise as he stepped forward, skirting a cane-bottomed chair, Buckner recognized it was Curly he was helping now, not himself. He thought virtuously: a woman couldn't find fault with this—helping a friendly man.

Curly jeered at Stafford: "The sheriff ain't jealous!"

Buckner sensed the final exploding spark in that. "Hold it!" he called urgently, and lunged for the steps.

Stafford's meaty cry of full-lunged anger overrode the words. "Drop him, boys!"

Fred Kistler's gun seemed instantly to lace the shadows with red bellowing spurts. Curly must have borrowed a gun and belt in the Eagle Bar. He fired almost as fast. And knew what he was doing. He had meant to do it when he took station there by the verandah, Buckner realized.

It was Stafford, clawing at his revolver, who took the full slam of Curly's heavy bullets. Stafford's bulk folded forward in grotesque jerks. From the top of the steps Buckner drove his shots at Kistler, trying to help Curly. He knew he was too late when Curly's gun went silent. A bullet tugged through his shirt sleeve. Roney Metcalfe was firing and backing away.

Buckner lunged down the steps, and that, and being alone now, broke Roney's nerve. He ran toward the corner of the hotel. With a regretful breath, Buckner let him go, and swung back to Curly.

He remembered and called to Adam Ingalls. "Two more are watching the back! They may get in this!"

Ingalls's rumbling decision urged the cattlemen in the lobby: "Enough of this! Help take over until the sheriff gets here!"

Curly was dead. In the yellow spurting match flare Buckner recklessly risked, Curly looked younger than ever. And somehow completely peaceful, as if Curly had found something which had been missing. Something Buckner had tried to tell him about in Black Cañon. A kind of self-respect a man could live with, or die with.

Buckner stood up and rolled a cigarette absently. The cattlemen were on the verandah with Adam Ingalls. In a moment or so it was plain that Tex and Red and Roney Metcalfe had decided that all this was Stafford's quarrel, and just about over now.

Buckner looked for a moment at men boiling out of the Eagle Bar or pounding across the dusty street and along the walks toward the trouble. Not a bad town, he thought. A man could back trail to worse towns and be less contented elsewhere. He saw Susan coming out and threw the unlighted cigarette away and started up the steps to tell her.

Acknowledgments

"Death for Double-O Neighbors" first appeared in *Ace-High Magazine* (9/37). Copyright © 1937 by Popular Publications, Inc. Copyright © renewed 1965 by Thomas Theodore Flynn, Jr. Copyright © 2018 by Thomas B. Flynn, M.D. for restored material.

"The Out Trail" first appeared in *The Popular Magazine* (2/31). Copyright © 1931 by Street & Smith Publications, Inc. Copyright © renewed 1959 by Thomas Theodore Flynn, Jr. Copyright © 2018 by Thomas B. Flynn, M.D. for restored material.

"Powder for Santa Anna" in *Argosy* (9/45). Copyright © 1945 by Frank A. Munsey Company. Copyright © renewed 1973 by Thomas Theodore Flynn, Jr. Copyright © 2018 by Thomas B. Flynn, M.D. for restored material.

"Hunted Wolf" first appeared in *Dime Western* (9/49). Copyright © 1949 by Popular Publications, Inc. Copyright © renewed 1977 by Theodore Thomas Flynn, Jr. Copyright © 1995 for restored material by Thomas B. Flynn, M.D. Reprinted by arrangement with Golden West Literary Agency. All rights reserved.

About the Author

T.T. Flynn was born Thomas Theodore Flynn, Jr., in Indianapolis, Indiana. He was the author of over 100 Western stories for such leading pulp magazines as Street & Smith's *Western Story Magazine*, Popular Publications' *Dime Western*, and Dell's *Zane Grey's Western Magazine*. He lived much of his life in New Mexico and spent much of his time on the road, exploring the vast terrain of the American West. His descriptions of the land are always detailed, but he used them not only for local color but also to reflect the heightening of emotional distress among the characters within a story. Following the Second World War, Flynn turned his attention to the book-length Western novel and in this form also produced work that has proven imperishable. Five of these novels first appeared as original paperbacks, most notably *The Man from Laramie* (1954) which was also featured as a serial in *The Saturday Evening Post* and subsequently made into a memorable motion picture directed by Anthony Mann and starring James Stewart, and *Two Faces West* (1954) which deals with the problems of identity and reality and served as the basis for a television series. He was highly innovative and inventive and in later novels, such as *Night of the Comanche Moon* (Five Star Westerns, 1995), concentrated on deeper psychological issues as the source for conflict, rather than more elemental motives like greed. Flynn is at his best in stories that combine mystery—not surprisingly, he also wrote detective fiction—with suspense and action in an artful balance. The psychological dimensions of Flynn's Western fiction came increasingly to encompass a confrontation with ethical principles about how one must live, the values that one must hold dear above all else, and his belief that there must be a balance in all things. The cosmic meaning of the mortality of all living creatures had become for him a unifying metaphor for the fragility and dignity of life itself.

Books are produced in the United States using U.S.-based materials

Books are printed using a revolutionary new process called THINKtech™ that lowers energy usage by 70% and increases overall quality

Books are durable and flexible because of Smyth-sewing

Paper is sourced using environmentally responsible foresting methods and the paper is acid-free

Center Point Large Print
600 Brooks Road / PO Box 1
Thorndike, ME 04986-0001 USA

(207) 568-3717

US & Canada:
1 800 929-9108
www.centerpointlargeprint.com